Texas Wedding Shoot-out . . .

The wedding party reached the platform and the preacher wasted no time beginning. Clint noticed right away that Milly looked faint and drugged. She was being supported by Rafe.

"What have they done to her?" Ben whispered.

"I don't know." Clint took a deep breath.

The preacher took courage as he neared the end of the marriage vows. "And so, if I hear no one who objects to this holy marriage between Mr. Rafus Longely and Miss Mildred Hathaway, I now pronounce you . . ."

"*I* object, you bloody bastard!"

All heads turned at the scream and they saw Della and her rifle. Della began to work the rifle as fast as she could lever it and pull the trigger. Men scattered in wild panic.

Clint and Ben alone sprinted toward the base of the wooden platform. Ben reached Milly first and tore the drugged and almost unconscious girl out of Rafe's arms as Della's rifle bullets screamed around them.

Clint saw Rafe's pistol come up and he braced himself for the killing bullet he knew he could not prevent . . . .

**Don't miss any of the lusty, hard-riding action
in the Charter Western series, THE GUNSMITH**

**And coming next month:
THE GUNSMITH #64:** THE FAST DRAW LEAGUE

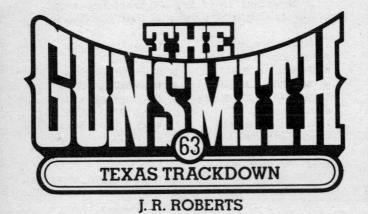

THE GUNSMITH

63

TEXAS TRACKDOWN

J. R. ROBERTS

CHARTER BOOKS, NEW YORK

THE GUNSMITH #63: TEXAS TRACKDOWN

A Charter Book/published by arrangement with
the author

PRINTING HISTORY
Charter edition / March 1987

ISBN: 0-441-30967-4

Charter Books are published by The Berkley Publishing Group,
200 Madison Avenue, New York, New York 10016.
PRINTED IN THE UNITED STATES OF AMERICA

ONE

It was a fine, midsummer day and the weather was a perfect seventy degrees as Clint Adams unlocked the door to his gun shop and opened for business. He was accustomed to plying his trade as a gunsmith out of the back of a wagon but, when a good friend offered him the free use of a small downtown shop, Clint decided to accept.

Santa Rosa, New Mexico, suited Clint right down to the ground. Nestled high in the lovely Sangre de Cristo Mountains, the small mining, ranching and freighting town was as peaceful and pretty as one would ever hope to find. It boasted a year-round population of about two thousand and they were, by and large, good upstanding people. There were big cattle ranches that generated a large payroll as well as some small gold and silver mining operations in the hills. Timber was plentiful and the town had a big sawmill down by the Lion River.

A couple of afternoons a week, Dade Evans and Clint would grab their fishing poles and catch trout.

"Mornin', Gunsmith!"

Clint looked up from the Winchester rifle he was fixing to see Dade step into his shop. "Mornin', Dade.

1

Can't take the afternoon off two days in a row, if that's what you came to ask.''

"Not even after the way the trout were bitin' yesterday?" Dade grinned mischievously. He was a smallish man, but a good one, and he had a refined sense of humor that Clint appreciated. Dade was fun to be around. He had a wife and three great kids. The whole family worked in their thriving general store.

"Not even," Clint said. "You come bringing me some business? How about that old Navy Colt you keep stuffed in that thing that barely resembles a holster? Why don't you trade it in on a decent piece of hardware? That thing is more likely to explode in your own face than do anybody else harm. This is the age of cartridges. I'm surprised that you can even buy black powder anymore for those relics.''

It was good-natured joshing, the kind that Clint enjoyed when he knew that he wasn't taken seriously.

"Hell," Dade growled, pulling out the old cap and ball and holding it up proudly. "This here pistol killed sixteen Comanches! Granddaddy swore by it. My paw once shot a mountain lion that was coming down on his back. Drilled that big cat right through the brainpan. This gun has never failed to serve the man who wore it. And since I'm the third generation of Evans men to pack it, I'm sure not about to change its luck.''

Clint knew there was a bottom-line seriousness about this. He had tried dozens of times to get Dade to at least let him recondition the old pistol. He would give it a good cleaning and check to make sure the antique still functioned.

"How long has it been since you cleaned the thing?"

Dade smiled. "Since the last time I shot it."

"And how long has that been?"

"About . . . oh, four years ago when I got drunk on the Fourth of July and plugged holes in the ceiling of the Bull Dog Saloon."

Dade Evans was about the mildest man Clint had ever met. It didn't seem possible he'd do such a thing but Clint had seen the bullet holes and heard the story at least four or five times. So it had to be true.

"Well," Clint said, "that means the gunbarrel is probably rusted or fouled so badly it'll explode in your face the next time you pull the trigger."

"Then I best stay sober on the Fourth of July, hadn't I," Dade said with a wink.

Clint shook his head. He gave up. This man often carried large amounts of money to the bank and really needed a modern piece of artillery on his hip. Clint, having won a reputation as a gunfighter and lawman, had even volunteered to teach Dade a thing or two about shooting. But the little merchant always got them headed off toward a good fishing hole instead.

"You sure I can't get you out after lunch?" Dade asked. "Hell, you're making too much money anyway!"

Clint laughed. It was a joke between them. Dade had a pretty and ambitious wife to stand behind the counter when he took the afternoon off. Mary Evans might grumble about her husband's easygoing ways and occasional shiftlessness, but she probably sold twice as much as Dade in the same amount of time. Mary was a real saleswoman. Dade just liked to talk so much that a customer was likely to walk out of his store and forget that he had come in to buy something.

Clint picked up the Winchester and pulled the trigger. Nothing happened. He was going to have to take the workings apart and replace a trigger spring. He knew it almost before he picked the rifle up. Clint understood guns better than horses or dogs, even. Much better than men and a hundred times better than women. Guns had been his life and livelihood for too many years not to have developed an affinity for them. He would no more go outside without a well-oiled and adjusted six-gun than he would with his fly unbuttoned.

"You sure got a lot of business in just the month you been in Santa Rosa," Dade said, his eyes scanning all the weapons Clint had in various stages of repair. "I never knew there was so damn much artillery in all of New Mexico. We could just about hold off the United States Army and the Apache."

Clint laughed. "Not quite. A lot of these are damn near as useless as the gun you wear. Others are so banged and bunged up they'll never shoot straight. It has always amazed me how a man will shine his boots to make them look pretty, but when it comes to his gun—a thing that can and will save his life—he won't even invest two bits for a can of gun oil and a good cleaning rag."

"Spoken like a true gunsmith."

"Get out of here," Clint growled with mock ferocity, "before I test one of these old double-barreled shotguns out on your backside."

"I'm leaving! I'm leaving!"

The door banged shut and Clint went back to work. In truth, he had gotten a lot more business than he'd ever expected. Maybe a man just did better when he got a little store and looked more permanent. Though working out of a wagon and traveling around the country fixing guns was a lot more fun and interesting. And come the tag end of summer, Clint reckoned he'd saddle up his big black gelding named Duke and hit the trail again.

It didn't pay for a man to spend too many months in the same town. Pretty soon, people started to think you were permanent. They'd begin to ask you your opinion on the town council, the mayor and whether or not the sheriff ought to be full-time or just part-time.

Hell, Clint thought as his fingers expertly dismantled the Winchester, the sheriff ought to be full-time! Right now he just comes in at noon and works until five, then goes back to his livery stable and feeds the horses before going home.

The day grew warmer as it passed. By early afternoon, Clint had finished with the rifle and two pistols. He was now replacing one of the hammers on a double-barreled shotgun. This was a mean weapon, one that had its barrels sawed off to get more scatter. Clint was a pistol man himself, but there were times when nothing could quite handle a bad situation like a shotgun.

Take that time in old Tuscosa, Colorado, he thought, as his strong fingers removed the screws holding the stock to the chamber, when eight outlaws had stepped into his office with the idea of killing him before they robbed the bank. Now, if he hadn't had a shotgun lying across his desk, well, sir, he'd have been dead meat. That shotgun said he could blow them all down with two barrels, or at least cripple them so badly they'd never escape. So the eight had looked right into those big double-barrels and seen the way things were without much conversation. They surrendered and he'd gotten two hundred dollars reward for the capture of Black Thumb Ernie and his men.

Without the shotgun, one just like the one he was fixing the hammer on, he'd have missed a whole lot of living and loving.

Clint looked up to see Dade leave his general store.

The Gunsmith smiled because Mary must have discouraged her husband from going fishing a second afternoon in a row. Clint watched the little merchant tip his hat to the prettiest woman in the county, Miss Milly Hathaway. Milly's father, Ace, owned the finest cattle spread in northern New Mexico. It was said to cover sixty thousand acres of the best range for miles around. Clint had never been on the Hathaway ranch, but he would if Milly ever asked him. She was a long-legged, strawberry blonde with an hourglass figure and a smile that would make an old man's toes curl. Clint had heard all the rumors about how old Ace would horsewhip any man foolish enough to look crossways at his only daughter. Maybe that was why Milly was twenty-three and still unmarried.

Milly glanced across the street and saw Clint watching her through the front window of his crowded little shop. Milly waved and Clint waved back hoping she might come pay him a visit. But she didn't and passed out of sight. Clint wasn't too disappointed. Milly liked his looks, he could tell that. And probably, she just had too many errands to run before the stores and bank closed.

Clint used only half his attention on the sawed-off shotgun. He had repaired guns so long that his hands automatically knew what was required. He whistled a little song he'd learned from a dancehall girl named Lola. Ahh, he remembered Lola very fondly. Now there was a woman for you, one who'd give even Milly Hathaway a race for the size and shape of her body and the warmth of her inviting smile. Lola, if he remembered exactly, had been singing to piano music and the first song he'd heard from her lovely throat had been . . .

Clint's reverie was shattered by the sound of gunfire. Without thinking twice, he tightened the last screw down on the shotgun, crammed two shells into it and lunged for the door and turned for the bank.

In a split second, he saw Dade Evans with that old cap and ball pistol in his hand. The merchant was staggering back into the street. Clint saw him raise the heavy weapon and try to fire it but nothing happened. The gun didn't shoot. But the four outlaws coming out of the bank more than made up for that damned old cap and ball pistol. They shot Dade three more times. Clint could see the small man's body jerk as each round struck home.

Clint shouted a warning in hopes of directing the outlaws' attention to himself. It worked, but it was too late. Dade was obviously dead before he hit the street.

Clint saw the outlaws spin and begin to fire at him. He dropped the shotgun and drew the well-oiled, perfectly adjusted and balanced Colt .45 Peacemaker on his hip. He fired as he began to run a zigzag pattern. His bullets screeched across the wide dirt street and two of the outlaws went down hard. Clint felt a bullet slice his cheek and he threw himself into the dirt. He raised his gun, shot another bank robber through the chest and watched him crash through the front window of the town's only barbershop.

Three down, only one to go. Clint rolled sideways and aimed, knowing he would not miss. But suddenly, Milly Hathaway appeared in his sights and then the last outlaw was throwing himself back inside the bank and slamming the door shut.

Clint rolled behind a water trough.

Time passed and nothing moved. Finally, a voice from inside the bank yelled, "Hey! You out there with the fast gun! You hear me?"

"Yeah!" Clint shouted.

"Then hear me good! I've got the money and the girl and we're coming out. I want safe passage out of this town or the girl is finished! You understand me?"

Clint cussed. He understood very, very well. And when the outlaw emerged with Milly right in front of him and with a gun pressed to her head, Clint knew he was in deep trouble.

"Hey, fast gun! You throw down your weapon and come on over here or I'll kill this woman!"

Clint cussed some more. He was a dead man if he obeyed the order, but Milly was a dead woman if he did not.

Damn! Clint pitched his gun out and slowly stood up. He expected a bullet right then but it didn't come.

"Walk on over here."

Clint walked. As he grew closer, he saw the crazed hatred in the outlaw's eyes. The man was going to try to get safely away, but not before he kills me, Clint decided.

That's as sure a bet as today's sundown.

TWO

"Move faster, damn you!" the outlaw raged. With a thick forearm locked across Milly's pretty throat, he yanked her up onto her toes and her face went red.

Clint wanted to lunge at the bandit and tear his head off but the gun aimed at his chest hinted that those kinds of thoughts were certain to get him killed.

"What do you want?" Clint said through gritted teeth.

"I want you to move on ahead of me and walk real slow and easy into that livery barn where you're going to get a horse saddled for me and the girl. Then, you're going to follow my directions or I'll blow your damned head off!"

Clint made himself smile just as if that all sounded peachy-fine. But inside, the Gunsmith was fuming that he hadn't grabbed a derringer instead of the damned shotgun. With a derringer, he could certainly find an opportunity to even the odds.

"Tell this town to hold their fire or you and the girl are both buzzard bait!" the bank robber bellowed. "Tell them to get off the street right now!"

Clint sighed. He filled his lungs and shouted, "Listen, everybody. This man is saying he won't put up with any heroics. And I won't be too damned pleased myself be-

9

cause he'll kill me along with Miss Hathaway. So everybody, just calm down and go back into your businesses or go home. Things will be alright.''

The townspeople who'd come to fight now lowered their guns, but they sure didn't look very cooperative. That wasn't too surprising considering the outlaw had a big canvas sack stuffed full of money slung over his shoulder—money that was everyone's life savings.

"Hold up there! This is the sheriff of Santa Rosa speaking. I demand that you drop your gun and release those people. And I ain't kiddin', Mister!''

Clint had not seen Big Jerome Wadmore step out of the livery with his gun in his hand. Now it was too late.

The outlaw knew he was hung if he gave up and surrendered. He pressed his gun to Milly's head and screamed, ''Talk to that big, stupid sonofabitch or this woman is finished! Tell him to throw down his weapon!''

Milly looked about ready to pass out and Clint didn't blame her one bit. Jerome Wadmore was the most obstinate, stubborn man in New Mexico.

No one had ever known him to change his mind on a single issue—not even the trivial stuff. And now, unless he backed down, there would be a lot of innocent blood spilled.

"Dammit, Jerome!'' the Gunsmith pleaded, walking ahead toward the man. ''You must listen to him and throw your gun down like he says.''

"Uh-uh,'' Jerome said, his big, square body hunched forward, massive arms and shoulders tensed. ''He gives up here and now. It's my job . . . I take the town's pay. I take all the responsibility.''

"But they only pay you ten dollars a month!'' Clint raged. ''That isn't enough to get us all killed.''

"It's enough."

Clint groaned. He didn't dare turn around because he knew he'd see stark terror on Milly's red face. Clint also knew that Jerome was a fool who was going to get them all killed in about five seconds if he wasn't taken care of at once.

"Listen, Jerome," he pleaded in desperation. "Could I talk to you for just one small second? I think I got us a way to settle this little fix we're all in."

Jerome shook his massive head. "I already know how to settle it. He drops the gun and lets Miss Milly go. He's got some of my fam'ly's money in that sack too, by gawd, and I ain't losin' it to no outlaw. Not me bein' the sheriff and all."

Clint made up his mind. He twisted around for a moment and winked at the outlaw just to let him know he had things in control. Then he walked right up to the huge blacksmith and placed a hand on Jerome's muscular shoulder and said, "Jerome, I tell you what I'm going to do."

"What are you goin' to do, Gunsmith?"

"This!" Clint hated like hell to do it, but he drove his knee into Jerome's crotch. Punching the man would probably just have busted his fist and started a bloodbath. So Clint just kneed him as hard as he could.

Big Jerome's cheeks blew out so far he looked like a squirrel with a mouth full of walnuts. His face drained of color and he said, "Ugggh!" and bent over.

That's when Clint grabbed Jerome's six-gun and twisted around with the speed of a cat. The bank robber was caught half-surprised but he still had time to fire. Clint howled as a bullet drilled him in the fleshy part of his right buttock.

He collapsed and fired when Milly bit the outlaw on

the arm and threw herself out of the line of fire. Clint's
gun blazed just as the outlaw unleashed his second bullet. Clint felt that bullet pluck his Stetson off his head.
But by then, Jerome's six-gun was bucking in his fist
and the outlaw was slowly backpeddling, watching bullets stitch holes across his chest. The last of the Santa
Rosa bank robbers died on his feet and crashed over a
hitching rail spilling money all over the place.

Clint dropped the six-gun in the dirt and collapsed to
his hands and knees. He reached around to grab his buttocks and when he pulled his hand away, it was covered
with blood. The Gunsmith swore in helpless fury. In all
his years as a lawman, he'd never been shot in the tail
end before—it was particularly galling to have it happen
before a girl as pretty as Milly Hathaway and an entire
town of gawking onlookers.

Jerome was still down, still cupping his privates
and looking greenish. "Goddamn you, Gunsmith," he
choked, "I'm going to take your head off for this!"

Clint blinked in amazement. "You big dumb ox!" he
raged. "Thanks to me, you just got a knee in the balls
instead of a bullet in the head! You owe me your life!"

But Jerome looked anything but grateful as he
crawled to his feet and staggered over to the dead outlaw. "It was my job to kill him, Gunsmith, not yours. It
was mine!"

Pretty Milly Hathaway brushed the dirt off her dress
and stabbed a shaky finger at the part-time sheriff.
"Jerome, you're dangerous! You would have gotten us
all killed and when Ace hears about how dumb you
acted, he's liable to come to town and horsewhip the
hide off of you!"

Jerome paled even more. Ace Hathaway was a huge,
mean old badger of a man who had skinned the flesh off

more than one man in his lifetime. He might be pushing seventy years old, but with a blacksnake in his gnarled paw, he was a force to be reckoned with. One might be able to shoot Ace Hathaway, but no man would ever beat him. Not even one as big as Jerome.

"But Miss Milly, please," Jerome begged, "I was doin' it for you! I couldn't let Ace's pride and joy get kidnapped from Santa Rosa by an outlaw. Your Pa, he'd have killed me."

"He may anyway," Milly said angrily.

She stooped down beside Clint and gazed deep into his eyes. "Gunsmith," she whispered, her voice going gentle as the murmur of pines in a soft breeze, "you got all four of them by yourself and you saved my life. I never seen a man that could fight the way you did! I've heard all the stories about you, but stories are mostly lies and I figured you couldn't be as brave and . . . daring as they said. But I was wrong. You're something special."

With her lovely face only inches away, Clint swallowed noisily and tried to think of something modest to say. But it turned out she didn't want to hear any words. She put her arms around his neck and kissed him deeply.

And kneeling there together in the dirt, with the dead outlaw, the pissed-off part-time sheriff and the whole damn town watching, Clint even forgot about the bullet buried deep in his throbbing buttocks.

THREE

It hurt like blazes to walk and it hurt a whole lot more to sit down. But what hurt most of all was when Dr. Cready dug the bullet out of his bleeding behind. That was about the most painful thing that Clint had ever endured and he was not to be faulted for screaming like a turpentined cat. When his howls got too loud, he asked for a stick and bit down hard enough to leave his fang marks.

"It was a bad one, Gunsmith, but I got it out. Want to keep it as a souvenir?"

Clint was lying flat on the operating table with his pants pulled down to his knees. It was a most embarrassing situation. There weren't many men who could retain any dignity under those circumstances, but he tried. "Doctor, a souvenir is the last thing that I want to remind me of this humiliation."

Dr. Cready was a thin, sickly-looking man in his midforties with watery blue eyes and a little goatee that reminded Clint of cornsilk. He cleared his throat and said, "Well, I'm sorry to hear you say that because the whole danged town of Santa Rosa is going to give you a whale of a celebration."

"Me?"

"Why, sure! You're a hero! Saved the entire town's life savings. Killed four bank robbers and saved Miss Milly's life . . . and Jerome's."

"The last part was pure accident," Clint groused. "That man is more dangerous than the outlaws."

"He tries. Jerome takes his responsibilities and that badge he wears very seriously. But never mind that. The main thing is that you are going to be feted by the entire town this Saturday afternoon."

"What does 'feted' mean?" Clint thought he knew, but it always paid to make sure when a highly educated man was laying big words on him.

"It just means you are going to be honored for your bravery and service to the community."

"Saturday is Dade Evans' funeral. I won't feel like celebrating, not with him dead. He was the brave one. Not me."

The doctor nodded. "Perhaps so. But the matter is settled. There will, of course, be some kind of glowing words said in tribute to poor Dade. He was universally liked and we'll miss him very much. But it was you—the Gunsmith—who saved Santa Rosa. If that outlaw had gotten away with our money, why, this town would have folded up its tent and died!"

Clint frowned. "I still wish you'd say something to whoever came up with this cockeyed idea."

"Why don't you tell her?"

"Her?"

"That's right. Miss Hathaway came up with the idea and her father, Ace, is going to bring two fat steers into town to butcher. Not that I'll believe that until I see it. Ace is a tightwad and a mean old skinflint. But there will be a rodeo, and later that night, a dance. Everybody is so damned relieved about still having their money, they just want to celebrate. The mayor is even going to give a speech.''

"Old Windy Wilson!"

"That's right," the doctor said. "I know, there goes the evening. But the town council is all het up over the idea and they're going to do it whether it pleases you or not. So you might as well be pleased and enjoy it. I imagine you've shot a good many men and risked your life with damn few thanks or rewards.''

"That was always part of the job.''

"Well, consider this part of our job." He finished the bandaging. "Going to be very, very sore for about three weeks. You'll have to sleep on your stomach and stay out of the saddle.''

"I will.''

The doctor inspected the graze wound along his cheek, and another across his ribs. "You sure are one lucky man," he said, his finger tracing out three more old bullet scars on Clint's back and sides. "How many times have you been shot?''

"Once too many," Clint said, grunting with pain as he slid off the table and dressed. "And I'll tell you something, I never want another slug in the butt. That was the most painful of all.''

"Lot of nerve endings and blood vessels. But no vital organs. Not on the back side, at least.''

He winked at Clint and washed his hands.

"How much do I owe you, Doc?''

"Not a damn thing. I had three thousand dollars in the bank. Without you, I'd have lost it all. Consider the debt paid in full.''

"Well, thanks.''

Clint hobbled outside and walked right into a big

crowd of well-wishers. They were all speaking at once, congratulating him and pounding him on the shoulder. If any of them pounded him low, he was going to howl like a catamount and start swinging.

"Alright, alright, fer chrissakes! Give the man some air!" They all shut up and Ace Hathaway, all six-foot-four and two hundred fifty-five pounds of him came struggling forward. Clint had never seen a man walk like Ace; he seemed as if he was tied together with barbed wire and the barbs were jabbing him at every move. He was all stoved up in the joints from fights and broncs and covered with scars and warts. The man just looked mean and cantankerous. And maybe, because his great frame had finally gone to hell, he had a right to be.

Ace wasn't a man known to be outwardly friendly, or friendly in any way, but now, he shoved out his massive hand and boomed, "Goddamn you, man, I owe you plenty much, by gawd!"

Clint stuck out his fist and immediately regretted it. The old New Mexico rancher towered over him, rough as the Sangre de Cristos themselves. "I just did what anyone would do, Mr. Hathaway."

"The hell you did!"

Clint managed to extricate his crunched hand without going white with pain.

"What you did, Gunslick . . ."

"Gunsmith," Clint corrected politely. "I'm called the Gunsmith. I like Clint even better."

The old man's massive jaw jutted out a little farther. "What you did, Gunslick, was to save this town and my little girl's life. I owe ya' fer that and I always pay my debts. Whatta you want? Money? Fine! Horses? Okay by me! Land . . . well, I reckon I'll even give you that.

Everything but my little Milly is yours fer the askin'. So go ahead and ask.''

"I don't want anything," Clint said. "Honest. I have enough money along with the fastest and best horse I ever saw.''

"What about land and cattle?''

"I'm not a cowman," the Gunsmith said. "I don't know much about roping or branding.''

"A man kin learn!''

Clint shook his head. He knew it was important for this man to give him something, but he'd be damned if he could think of what it might be. "How about some of your business?" he said finally. "Maybe you have a few guns around the ranch house that I could fix or adjust the workings on?''

"You wanna work for my thanks?''

"That's right," Clint said. "Your thanks are enough by themselves. And if you have any business, that'll even be better.''

The old cattleman and pioneer nodded. "I'll keep ya busy," he vowed, making it sound almost like a threat.

The mayor of the town finally worked up the courage to move in between them. He pumped Clint's hand up and down and said, "Mr. Adams, we have a real ripsnorter of a celebration planned in your honor. We sure do. We're all taking up a collection and . . . ''

"No.''

The mayor blinked. "Pardon me, sir?''

Clint repeated himself. "I said no. Any collections you get will go to the Evans widow and her family.''

"But . . . but they'll do fine! That store of theirs is a gold mine and . . . ''

Clint had heard enough. He tipped his hat to the mayor's wife and hobbled away from the doctor's office wanting nothing more than to be left alone for awhile. It wasn't that he didn't appreciate what these fine people had in their hearts, but he'd miss Dade Evans a lot and he'd miss the great afternoons they'd shared fishing and swapping lies.

Fishing. Clint decided right then that that was what he needed to do, just go off by himself beside the Lion River and do some fishing, not caring if he caught anything or not. He would fish and think about brave, foolish little Dade with his "good-luck" old family relic of a gun that failed and got him killed.

Hell, Clint thought, even with my gun Dade would have gotten shot the way he charged that bank like the Third Cavalry attacking Indians. It wasn't the old Navy Colt's fault and it wasn't even mine for not insisting I fix and clean it. It was the outlaws' faults.

And I killed the bastards. And that's all there is to the story. That's all.

FOUR

Clint hobbled over to his hotel room and everyone in town who saw him called out in greeting. People smiled and repeated his name or just yelled, "God bless you, Gunsmith," as he passed. Most everyone tried to pat his shoulder. Clint had rid the West of a lot of bad men, but he had never seen such a public outpouring of appreciation as he was receiving from the citizens of Santa Rosa. It didn't make his poor, aching fanny feel any better, but it sure raised his spirits.

When he approached the Bull Dog Saloon, four good-looking dancehall girls stepped out onto the boardwalk. One, named Rosie, extended a bottle of champagne and then threw her arms around his neck and gave him a powerful hug. She was big and busty and wore enough perfume to ward off horseflies. It was a struggle just to break free.

"We'd like you to come inside and share this with us, Clint darlin'! We want to give you a private party up in our rooms that you'll never forget."

Rosie winked. "We've drawn straws on who is going to thank you first, you handsome sucker you. I won! Before we're finished with you, honey, you'll think you died and went to heaven!"

Clint shook his head. "I can't," he said, trying to return the huge bottle of expensive French champagne and extricate himself from Rosie's grasp.

"Well, why not?"

"I'm wounded," Clint said, turning half around and showing them the lump of bandages that made his britches protrude like he was carrying a toad in his back pocket. "I took a bullet."

Rosie measured the damage and then proved she wasn't a woman who gave up easy. "Oh hell, that don't matter! Long as they didn't shoot off anything on your front side!"

The girls wailed with coarse laughter. Clint appreciated their generous intentions but he wanted to be alone. Not only was his buttock aching like a bad tooth, but he wasn't in the mood for partying, not with Dade having been killed less than two hours before.

"Maybe some other time," he said, trying to be nice, yet firm.

But Rosie was insistent. "Aw, come on Clint! We're going to show you such a good time you'll forget all your pain. And you don't have to worry about any more damage. You'd best believe we girls know how to ride a lame horse as well as a sound one!"

More wild gales of ribald laughter.

Clint was starting to get annoyed. "I'll see you ladies some other time. And thanks for the champagne, I can use it," he said, trying to move around the women.

But two of them grabbed his arms and, just when he'd had all he could stand and was in danger of losing his temper, a voice snapped, "Get away from him, all of you!"

They spun around to see Miss Milly Hathaway. Her

face was pale with anger. She was sitting alone in a
buckboard, holding a buggy whip poised as if to strike.
The saloon girls retreated. Even Rosie appeared to be
thoroughly intimidated. "Miss Hathaway, we was just
trying to reward the Gunsmith in the only way we know
how. We didn't mean no harm."

Milly took a deep breath. Her lips were pressed tightly
together and her eyes flashed. "I know. I heard everything. Now get back into the saloon and give this man
some peace."

Rosie's cheeks flushed pink. She opened her mouth
but then clamped it shut again. "Remember," she whispered to Clint, "I got you first, honey."

Clint nodded. He had not taken his eyes off Milly
Hathaway. When they were alone, he went to tip his
Stetson and then remembered it had been shot off his
head. So he just said, "Thank you, Miss Hathaway."

She relaxed. "You look pretty done in, Clint. You
look . . . you look like a man who has earned a little
time by himself." She twisted around in the seat and
pointed to a shiny new fishing pole and reel. "I heard
you were going fishing and just now I rushed over to the
general store. I bought you some new tackle, a fishing
box, everything you'll need. I also picked up your old
Stetson and replaced it with a new one. The best they
had. I was in such a hurry, I hope it'll fit alright. If it
doesn't you can take it back."

He took the new Stetson she held out for him. Like
his old one, it was black, stiff and shaped just the way
he liked. "It's a perfect fit. A lot nicer hat than the ven-
tilated one."

"It's nothing compared to saving my life. And you
did save it, Clint."

He couldn't deny the fact and so he just shrugged.

"Clint? I can give you a lift over to the Lion River. It's too far to walk and you're in no shape to ride your horse. I brought a couple of blankets for you to lie on. How does that sound?"

"Best offer I've had all day," he said, moving to the back of the buckboard and gingerly climbing into the bed and rolling onto his stomach.

"Even better than Rosie's offer?" Milly asked as she started out of town.

Clint closed his eyes and relaxed. It was a warm day and he was not accustomed to riding in such comfort or being driven about by the prettiest woman in the whole territory. "Yeah, even better than Rosie's," he said. "You sure scared the daylights out of those girls with that little buggy whip."

Milly laughed happily. "It wasn't me that scared them! It was my father. He'd tar and feather the lot of them before running them out of town if he heard they talked back to me."

"I see. Isn't there anyone that is not afraid of your father?"

She thought about it for quite a while. "Nope. Just you and me, Clint. That's all."

"What about your brother, Jepson?"

"He's scared to death of Pa. Pa is ten times the man at seventy than Jepson is at twenty-three."

Clint frowned. He had heard that old Ace Hathaway didn't have much use for his handsome, but wastrel son. Clint had seen young Hathaway any number of times and he was always either drunk, or being hung onto by a couple of painted women. Jepson Hathaway was not a fine and upstanding young man. He had shifty eyes, a pasty face and was extremely cocky. Jepson seemed to fancy himself a gambler, lady-killer and gunfighter all rolled into one package.

"There is one other man who isn't afraid of Pa," Milly said after a while.

"Who's that?"

"Rafe Longely, our foreman. He isn't afraid of anything on earth. Maybe that's why he's the only man that can work for Pa. He'll stand up and speak his mind even if he knows what he has to say won't make Pa happy."

Clint had seen Rafe. The man was tall, angular and dangerous. It was said he had killed more than a few men down in Texas, but those were rumors. Nothing to put stock in. Clint had also heard that Rafe coveted Milly Hathaway and was just waiting for the chance to marry her and cash in on all the Hathaway land, cattle and money.

"Clint, have you met Rafe?"

"I've seen him around." Clint had seen the man bully and then whip three cowboys from another spread with ruthless efficiency.

"What do you think of him?"

"I have no opinion of him. Is he a good cattleman and foreman?"

His question caught her by surprise. "Well, well yes. Of course. He knows almost as much as Pa about cattle. He is an all-around top hand and he can control the men when Pa is feeling bad. Pa says Rafe is the most capable foreman he's ever seen. Rafe looks after our ranch almost as well as if he owned it. Trouble is, he sort of acts like he owns me, too."

She twisted around. "I don't want to be owned by any man, Clint. I just want to be married and a partner to a man. Rafe doesn't seem to want to hear what I think about cattle and ranching. I guess he figures he knows enough already. Do you?"

Clint looked up at her. "Do I know enough about cattle and ranching?"

"Yes."

"Milly, what I know about ranching and cattle wouldn't cover a matchbox. I don't make any pretense of ever having been anything but a lawman and a gunsmith. It's plenty tough enough doing those two jobs well."

"I'd love to teach you about ranching," she said with a wide smile. "I never had anyone to teach, there's always been someone teaching me. I'm sort of tired of being talked down to and told how things ought to be."

"I can understand that," Clint said. "I never thought of it much, but it's a lot more fun to be a teacher than a pupil."

She pulled up beside the river and bent over to look at him. Twisted around like she was and being large-breasted, she looked ready to pop out of her blouse. "Is there anything at all you could teach me besides guns and how to shoot bank robbers?" she purred.

Clint swallowed. This was a virgin girl, he knew that sure as he knew that anyone who even looked cross-eyed at her would get skinned to death by old Ace Hathaway.

"I can . . . well," he said, very gingerly sliding out of the buckboard, "I can teach you how to fish."

"Shucks," she muttered. "I already know that!"

Clint hobbled down to the grassy riverbank not saying a word. He hoped Milly would leave him alone but he had a feeling she would not. Something in her eyes told Clint she wanted him to teach her a thing or two, but fishing had nothing to do with the first lesson.

FIVE

She spread the blankets out on the bank for him to
ease down upon and then she brought out all the new
fishing equipment for him to rig up.

"This is the nicest gear I ever used," Clint said with
admiration.

"It ought to be, it cost eighty dollars."

Clint blinked. "Eighty dollars!"

"And that didn't include the worms. But that doesn't
matter. As long as you are happy, Clint."

He got everything rigged up and then chose a fishing
hook and weights. "This river is pretty fast," he said.
"You have to add enough weight to get the worm near
the bottom."

"I know," she said. "I fished this spot a hundred
times if I've done it once."

"Oh." Clint chose a worm, baited it and then made
his cast from a sitting position. The hook did not go
very far and he was displeased. "I'll never catch anything if I can't get it out in the middle."

"Let me do it," she said, taking the pole and reeling
in the hook. She looked out at the current, seemed to
decide the perfect spot and then made a sensational cast,
one he could not have matched in distance. The worm

sank from sight and before she could even give him his new fishing pole, Milly had a strike.

"Wow!" Clint yelled, watching his shiny pole almost double on itself. "You must have a huge one! Go ahead and reel him in!"

"You sure?"

"Hell, yes! Hurry, before he gets away."

Milly laughed. "He isn't going anywhere, Clint. Not the way I set the hook."

And Milly was right. She reeled a whopper right up to the bank and then expertly flipped it up onto the grass where Clint unhooked it. "Milly," he said, "I've been fishing here a dozen times and never caught one this big."

"Just lucky," she said, kneeling down beside him and studying the fish. "If you're hungry, I bet I could rustle up a few branches and we could roast him over the fire. He'd go beautifully with that champagne."

Clint smiled and drew out his knife to clean the fish. "Best idea I've heard all day."

It was late afternoon and all that was left of the huge fish and one of its friends was a pile of bones. The French champagne was getting low too, but it had been fantastic. And now, as Milly pitched a few more sticks onto the fire, Clint felt like a new man. He looked up at the beautiful girl beside him who had grown very quiet.

"What are you thinking, Milly?"

"That I'd like to take a cool swim."

"Oh."

"Clint, would you mind? I mean, you're not in a hurry or anything, are you?"

"Nope, but . . . " What was she going to wear!

"Good. Then I'll swim. Wish you could join me."

"So do I. But I'll pass. Where are you going, upriver or down?"

Turning to look at him she said, "Neither. I'm going swimming right here. It's the best place to swim, Clint."

He took a deep breath. "I'm not sure your father would appreciate this."

"But he's not here." Milly turned her back to Clint as she unbuttoned her blouse and then removed her bra. Clint watched dry-mouthed as she stood up and slipped out of her underclothes right down to her bare skin. His hands began to shake a little as he studied the beautiful turn of her buttocks and, when she swayed down to the water, he had to close his eyes or he knew he was going swimming too.

She'll get you horsewhipped, tarred and feathered, he told himself again and again as he lay down and closed his eyes. Ignore her!

"Clint! Help!"

He was on his feet in an instant. She was in water over her head and going under. Clint pitched off his Stetson, gunbelt and boots and dove in after her. He ignored the pain in his buttocks as he swam powerfully to save her. She seemed dazed and helpless and he had a tough time getting her to a narrow sandbar jutting out of the river.

"Milly, if you couldn't swim, why'd you go in over your fool head?"

She opened those lovely eyes of hers. "Because I was faking so you'd come in and save me twice in the same day," she murmured, raising her arms up and sliding along his body until her big breasts were dripping water in his face.

Clint stared at them for a moment. The nipples were chilled and hard. He raised his head and took one of them in his mouth. Milly sighed and hugged him tightly as his tongue began to move around and around over them. First one nipple and then the other. She groaned with pleasure and worked loose his belt.

"Milly," he whispered, knowing this was going to cause him grief. "You're a virgin and I'm not the kind of . . ."

She took his manhood in her cool hand and he forgot whatever it was he was going to say as she gently peeled off his trousers. He was the one who ripped away the doctor's soggy bandage from his own tail end.

"I want you to teach me this, Clint. Be a good teacher for me, please!"

He found himself nodding. His fingers slipped down the length of her long, supple body and when they found the nub of her pleasure, she shuddered with delight. He used his forefinger to bring her to a climax that had her heels furrowing the sandbar as she moaned and cried with animal pleasure.

"Now," she panted, her eyes glazed as she reached down and grabbed his rigid staff, "make me your woman!"

Clint felt her hand pull him down to her slick wetness and his last reservations vanished. He laid her down on the sandbar and moved on top of her. He hunched his hips forward and she stiffened and then grunted in pain. But when he tried to pull back, she bit his shoulder and grabbed his good buttock and pulled him deep into her.

"Ohhh, Clint!" she squealed as he began to rotate his hips and pump her, "I never dreamed it was so good!"

He lifted himself up on his elbows and gazed down into her lovely face. "Honey," he grunted as his body slowly began to pick up the tempo, "it's going to get a whole lot better before I'm through."

Clint played her like a musical instrument until her entire body was twanging as tight as a bowstring. And when he finally abandoned his eroding willpower and began to reach a thundering climax, Milly Hathaway was splashing and waving her hands and legs in the water, raising a huge ruckus. Clint's body stiffened and he drove himself in all the way as he filled her with his hot, spewing seed.

Milly's cries of delight gradually died as did her soft, puppy-like whimpering. They lay entwined like two lovers until the sunset lit up the sky.

"I love you, Clint," she whispered, "and I'll make you a better wife than you ever dreamed any woman could be."

Clint swallowed noisily. He was going to have to let her down slowly, but out here in the middle of Lion River was not the place to do it. She might just drown him. Milly was innocent and beautiful, but he was beginning to see that she was a very strong-willed girl, a real wildcat.

"I never dreamed the man I'd marry would be a real hero. Someone who'd save my life twice in the very same day. Oh, my darling, I'm so happy! Aren't you?"

She hugged him fiercely and ground her pelvis hard against his because she wanted to make love again.

"I'm downright delirious, Milly," he said as their bodies spoke to each other. "Nowhere I'd rather be."

And, for the moment at least, it was the truth.

SIX

It was almost sundown and Clint was just getting ready to hop back into the buckboard when Jepson Hathaway and Rafe Longely came charging up on their sweating horses.

"You'd better let me do the talking," Milly said, her face suddenly pinched with worry. "Thank heavens they didn't come by an hour ago!"

"You can say that again," Clint replied fervently. He made sure his belt was notched and his gun was in easy reach. As the two cowboys skidded their horses to a halt, it was easy to see that they were mad. Young Jepson Hathaway snapped, "Goddammit, Milly! We been looking for you everywhere. What the hell are you and him doing here?"

"We've been fishing."

"Fishin'!" he spluttered, his eyes darting over to their smoldering campfire and the pile of fishbones. "Well . . . why the hell you doin' a dumb thing like that! Pa was askin' where'd you go."

"It wasn't Pa," Milly said angrily. "It was you, Rafe. You got to learn someday that you don't own me. I won't be held accountable to you every time I want to visit another man! Besides, I've decided I'm going to marry the Gunsmith."

Clint groaned loudly. "Now Milly, I never said . . ."

"Shut your mouth!" Rafe bellowed. His lip twisted into a bitter scowl and his cheeks were so red and puffed out it looked as if he had a bone stuck in his throat and couldn't catch his breath. "You damn sure ain't marrying a nothing sonofabitch like him. Your pa wants you to marry a cattleman like me."

"I wouldn't marry you if you were the only man on the face of the earth. I love Clint!"

"Now, Milly," Clint said. "I think . . ."

"Shut up!" Rafe said, jumping down from his horse and striding over to them. "You keep your mouth shut or I'll shove my fist down your throat."

Clint knew he was in no condition to whip this man in a fistfight, but no man could talk to him or to a lady that way. Clint stepped back from the buckboard. "I think you owe me and Miss Hathaway an apology," he said, his voice as soft as a whisper.

"No!" Milly cried, stepping between them. "I won't have you two fighting over me. Rafe, I'm sorry. I didn't want to hurt you but I'm in love with Clint."

"Love! You don't even know the man. You're just . . . well, goddammit, I'd have saved your life too if I'd have been there. Right now, that's clouding your mind. He's no damn good for you."

Clint had heard about enough. "That's not for you to decide," he said.

Rafe climbed back into the saddle where he sat gripping his saddle horn with his big hands until his knuckles turned white. "Milly, you'd better come home," he said in a voice that sounded like dried leaves being trampled. "I think you been swimming and maybe you done something here I better know about with that man."

Rafe's deepset little eyes swung to Clint and pinned

him like a bug on a specimen board. Clint stiffened and
said, "We swam and ate. That's all you need to know,
Longely."

"I'll be the judge of that."

"No," Clint said, "I will."

Rafe started to get down again but Milly shouted,
"No! You stay in the saddle! We're going back to town
right now."

"You better be," Jepson said, his voice blustering
now that he could see the fear in his sister. "Pa will hear
about you and him."

Clint had to bite his own tongue. He had no desire
to get into a fight with anyone. He'd done more than
enough killing for one day and, besides, young Hathaway was all show. Hurting him would accomplish nothing and make life miserable for all of them. But this
Rafe was another matter entirely. Clint knew the man
was boiling inside, held in check only by Milly, not by
Clint and his reputation.

Clint studied the man. Their eyes locked. Clint said,
"I'm not getting up on this buckboard until you and
Jepson ride along. We won't be herded into town like
sheep. So decide what you want to do right now."

"Rafe . . . "

The tall, powerful ramrod of the Hathaway ranch
turned at Milly's sharp warning. Then, after a long moment, he began to rein his sweaty horse back toward
Santa Rosa. But first he said, "Gunsmith, you're a big
man in town right now. A hero to Miss Hathaway and
all the rest. It wouldn't do for me to shame or even
shoot a hero, now would it?"

"A man has to do what he has to do," Clint said.
"I'll be around."

Rafe looked over his shoulder as he rode away. "I'm

glad to hear that. Just don't let me find you around
Miss Hathaway like this again."

"Rafe, dammit!" Milly cried. "Don't you understand, we are getting married!"

"Over my dead body," he roared as he touched spurs
and galloped back toward town.

Jepson watched the big man until he disappeared
and then said, "Milly, you're gonna get someone killed
here. You want that on your conscience?"

She looked up at her older brother. "Go back to your
saloon girls and leave us alone. And do yourself a favor
and stay away from Rafe. He's leading you where you
don't want to go."

Jepson blinked and then stabbed a finger at Clint.
"Rafe has it straight, Gunsmith. You ain't marrying
into the ranch. You think you found a home, think
again."

"Go home, boy."

Jepson cursed him, then yanked his horse around and
spurred hard after Rafe. Clint shook his head and
frowned. He looked over at Milly who seemed very worried. "Come here," he said.

She went into his arms and he could feel her shaking
with anger or fear—maybe it was both. "You alright?"
he asked.

She nodded. "You don't know how bad it is living on
the ranch with a brother like that and Rafe. He's always
watching me, kind of like I was something to eat. Once
in a while, some poor cowboy new on the payroll will
look sideways at me and the next thing I know, Rafe has
beaten him half to death and sent him packing."

"You ever talk to your father about it?"

"No," she confessed. "If I did, I'm afraid of what
might happen."

"Your father would kill his own foreman?"

She shook her head. It was damned obvious that Milly was worried the ranch foreman would kill old Ace. She looked up at him. "Will you marry me, Clint?"

"I just can't."

"But . . . " tears welled up in her eyes. "After what we did together . . . oh, Clint, I do love you!"

He took her into his arms and cradled her head against his chest. "Milly, I told you how I feel about marriage. I thought you understood."

"But I'd make a wonderful wife for you! You'd be so happy. And I'm worth a lot of money."

He had to smile. "You're worth more than money. That's why someday a fine man will ask to marry you and he won't give a damn about the money or the ranch."

She sniffled. "But you're the only man in the world that could stand up to both my father and Rafe. Anybody else would run! Don't you see, not only am I in love with you, but you're my only chance for marriage and happiness?"

Despite the circumstances, the Gunsmith had to agree there was more than a little truth in what she was saying. Rafe would kill or beat any other suitor and old Ace still considered Milly to be his baby. Unless Clint missed his guess, the rancher would not welcome anyone—no matter how sincere or successful—as a suitor for Milly.

"Clint, please! Give us a chance. Don't say no so easily. I want to make love to you every day right here by the river. And if you can still say you don't want me and love me after a month, then you can forget me and I swear I won't beg or even blame you."

"Milly," he said, "we couldn't get away with this

everyday. And . . . well, dammit, none of this is fair to you. You need to be courted. Brought flowers to and danced with. You deserve better than to sneak down here by the river and try to win something like that. When you make love with a man, it has to be because you want to—not because you're trying to trap him into marrying you."

"I've failed," she said miserably. "It's clear now that I don't know anything about love. You must think me a silly young girl without pride or even any good sense."

Clint felt awful. "How old are you?"

"Twenty-three," she told him. "Around here, that's old for a girl to still be single and unheard of to be a virgin unless you are a fright. Until you came along and saved my life, I was starting to wonder if I would ever be made into a woman."

"You already were a woman. A lot of woman."

"What good is expensive wine if the bottle is never opened?"

She had him on that one. "Listen," he said, knowing he couldn't desert her in this state and leave her at the mercy of Rafe Longely, "why don't we see each other awhile?"

Her face brightened and she hugged him fiercely.

"Oh, Clint! I knew you'd come around. Where can we meet where no one will see us making love?"

"I think we ought to meet in the open and stop making love," he said reluctantly. "I know I'm going to kick myself for saying this, but we need to become friends. Who knows, maybe it's time I learned something about ranching."

"I'll teach you everything!" She kissed him passionately. "And I'll show you all the most beautiful places that I know in these mountains. We'll have fun together."

He was glad to see her smile in the twilight. "Alright. And will you show me all the best fishing holes? And teach me to cast a line the way you do?"

"Well, sure! And how to throw a rope, brand a cow and . . ."

"Whoa up," he said, touching his backside. "You forget, I'm a wounded man."

She reached around and rubbed his bottom very tenderly, then winked like a vixen. "I didn't forget. And that's why I was easy on you today!"

Clint laughed at that, and, for the moment at least, it was easy to forget about Rafe and the hatred Clint was sure would soon lead to a deadly gunfight.

SEVEN

Dade Evans' funeral was a well-attended social event. The mortician spared no expense in making everything as fine as possible and the preacher gave an exceptional funeral service. The day was cloudy, the skies almost an indigo blue. Clint was dressed in his only suit, his hair was freshly cut and his jowls were cleanly shaved.

Mrs. Evans had asked Clint to be one of the pallbearers and he felt especially honored. There were piles of flowers and Clint could not help thinking how, when it came his time to cash it in, he'd be lucky to have ten good men and women friends. Dade had dozens.

When the funeral was over, Clint waited beside the grave until most of the people were headed back to town. Then, he paid his respects to his late friend's family and offered them any help he could.

"You were help enough when Dade was alive," Mrs. Evans said. "I don't imagine he told you, but Dade was so proud you were his friend. Proud enough to bust."

"He was?"

"Yes. A man as famous and brave as you, taking up with a storekeeper."

"I was the one that was lucky."

"I know that," the woman said, "but Dade never

did. He was the most unassuming, modest person I've ever known. What are you going to do now, Clint?"

"Stick around awhile. Then I'll move on."

The widow lifted her black veil to glance over at Rafe and Jepson who had remained near the cemetery gate. "Just be careful of those two men. They're as evil as rattlesnakes and twice as dangerous."

Clint put his new Stetson back on his head and nodded. "I know that. And I'll be careful."

He left the widow with her children and her grief and then he went to the Hathaway coach and shook hands with Ace. "Sir," he said, "with your permission, I'd like to come visit your daughter."

The craggy rancher stared down at him. "For what purpose?"

"I don't rightly know for sure," Clint said honestly. "Except to say that she needs to have a man as a friend. She has a wonderful father and brother, but she needs a friend."

Whatever the rancher had been about to say was forgotten. "You saved her life the other day," he said. "You got the right to visit any damned time you want. There will be no trouble over it, ain't that right, Rafe?"

The foreman had been close enough to overhear everything. "Yes, sir," he said stiffly. "But I told you what your daughter said about marrying the sonofabitch."

Clint had to fight to keep from turning on the foreman. But losing his temper in this place and killing Rafe would be a shock and intrusion on the grieving Mrs. Evans and her children.

"I know what the hell you said!" Ace snapped, "and I told you I'd handle things. Jepson, same goes for you. You boys understand that?"

They nodded and marched toward their horses.

"Gunsmith, you're a man that has known a few women. Good and bad. Ain't that right?"

"Yes."

"Then you know that my Milly is . . . sweet as sugar and untried. She ain't ready for marriage yet."

"But I'm twenty-three years old, Pa!"

The man swung around and it was easy to see that he had to struggle to hold his temper. "You let me handle this," he grated. "Gunsmith, you did save her life, but I won't have you diddlin' around and messin' her up. Hear me?"

"I hear you."

"Good!" Ace Hathaway relaxed and took up the reins of his team. "Then if you understand that, we will get along jest fine. Now, there's to be a celebration and I did send along two steers yesterday which Rafe butchered. So let's go down and eat some of the best beef in New Mexico and have us a high old time."

Clint smiled. "Can I have the first and last dance with your daughter?"

Ace snapped his buggy whip and the coach jerked away, but not before he yelled, "Hell yes, Gunslick, you're the guest of honor today!"

Clint headed for his black gelding. He wasn't looking forward to being feted and praised, but that was beyond his control. So he'd just try to make the best of it, have his dance with Milly and try to forget about poor Dade Evans.

Dade would not have minded his friend the Gunsmith having a few drinks and a little pleasure on his burying day. And if they'd talked about Milly Hathaway, he'd have told Clint to go ahead and court the girl. Milly needed him and maybe Clint would discover he needed a fiery young girl like Milly on a permanent basis.

But I'll never make a real cowboy, Clint thought as he watched two of the cowhands race their ponies toward town, whooping and already raising hell. It just isn't my style.

EIGHT

As Clint was escorted into the Bull Dog Saloon, a packed crowd burst into cheers and salutes.

"Oh, Christ no," Clint swore soft enough that no one could hear him. Not being the kind of man who enjoyed being made a hero, he would have retreated right then and there except that the crowd closed off his escape route.

Rosie shoved her way forward and threw her arms around his neck hard enough to put a crick in it. She squealed in his ears and then mashed his lips and the crowd roared with delight.

"Give the poor man some air, Rosie!" the crowd yelled as Clint struggled to break free.

The mayor yanked out his pistol and emptied it into the heavy crystals dangling off a huge chandelier. The crowd ducked as flying glass rained down upon them and someone twisted the gun out of the fool's hand.

"Ladies and gentlemen!" the mayor roared. "And I do use those terms loosely."

It was the oldest opening line in the world and it still worked as the crowd howled with delight.

"I want to be the first of many to buy the hero of Santa Rosa a drink this afternoon. And in one hour we will all crawl out of here and take to the podium for the speeches.''

Everyone groaned. The mayor was famous for his long-winded speeches. And the really bad news was that there were several men on the town council who could and always did give him a close run for his money.

''Drinks on the house!'' the owner of the saloon bellowed. ''Step right up here and belly up to the bar!''

Clint felt a surge of human bodies move toward the bar but the floor was so packed that few could get their free drink. After that, everyone paid except him. They kept his glass full and though he was not known as a rounder, he was feeling no pain when they finally gathered him up on their shoulders and marched down Main Street.

Clint relaxed as best he could and figured he might as well enjoy the moment. In all his years of being a tough lawmaker, he had never been so appreciated. But then, neither had he ever saved an entire community's savings.

They came to a hangman's gallow and carried him right up to the top of the damned thing. He looked up and was appalled to see an empty hangman's noose waving ever so slightly in the soft afternoon breeze.

''I'd appreciate it if you'd have someone grab that thing and haul it down,'' Clint said, as they placed him in the seat of honor right over the trap door. Clint could feel the trap door sag a little when it took his weight. After sending so many outlaws and misfits to the gallows, Clint did not like the idea of being in such a tenuous position.

The mayor cleared his throat three or four times, filled his chest and bellowed, ''Ladies and gentlemen—

and I do use those terms loosely!''

It worked all over again, Clint observed with a shake of his head. Even the kids squealed with mirth.

''Ladies and gentlemen, it gives me the greatest honor of my illustrious political career to present to you a legend of a man. Some know him merely as the polite, softspoken Clint Adams, but to many others, he is known as the famous Gunsmith. A man who, during just one exciting decade of dangerous duty, has single-handedly killed over one hundred outlaws!''

The crowd cheered wildly. Young men placed their forefingers into their mouths and tested each other to see who could whistle the loudest. Women stared at him with a mixture of admiration and fear. Kids fell silent and their mouths dropped open as they craned their necks to see the deadly six-gun he wore. Clint just pulled his Stetson down low on his forehead and wanted to be elsewhere. A hundred men—for chrissakes! The mayor was a shameless exaggerator. It could not have been over thirty or so—every one of whom deserved to die.

The mayor was starting to catch his stride. ''I remember the first time I saw the Gunsmith in action. It was in Dodge City and he faced sixteen outlaws all alone at sundown. And when his smoking six-gun was empty . . . ''

''There were still ten or eleven of 'em left standing and he'd run out of bullets!'' a heckler shouted. ''Sit down and shut up, Mayor. Let the Gunsmith tell his own lies!''

The mayor blushed hotly as that cry was taken up by the mass of spectators. He was smart enough to know when it was time to close his mouth and wait for another day and a gentler crowd. But he had to finish his story and salvage a little of his dignity.

"And so . . . he killed them all with the other two guns he carried and then he rode out of Dodge City without expecting—or receiving—any show of gratitude whatsoever."

"I never shot and killed but two men in Dodge City," Clint said to no one in particular.

The mayor pretended not to hear. "And so . . . that is why it gives me such great pleasure to see all you good people joining me in saluting this great gunfighter who has saved our bacon and bank. Ladies and gentlemen, I give you . . . the Gunsmith!"

Clint was shoved to his feet. The sun was shining brightly and he had drunk too much whiskey. He stared out at the faces of the crowd. These were nice, hard-working people. Family people with sunburnt faces, blond-haired little kids and the look of honesty in their eyes. Eyes that were frankly shining with admiration.

Clint knew he had to say something to express what he-felt and so he took a deep breath. He spotted pretty Milly Hathaway and spoke mainly to her.

"What I did the other day here in the street wasn't so brave. You see, I was just doing what I have trained myself to do in order to stay alive. I shot fastest and truest because I have killed more men than I care to remember. You young boys, don't stare at my six-gun and dream of becoming a gunfighter. Men like me will pass out of history before long. The law won't always be that of the six-gun. People will civilize the West and make it a safe place to live. I guess that there will always be outlaws and there might be need for a few men handy and quick with a pistol. But I would like to think otherwise."

He looked to the widow, Mary Evans, and her children. "Mrs. Evans, Dade was the real brave one. He

charged the bank knowing he was no match for all those
gunmen. He died as courageously and as well as any
man I've ever known. If it hadn't been for him, I
wouldn't have heard the gunshots and they'd probably
have gotten away scot-free. It was Dade who did what
had to be done to save the bank—not me."

The crowd turned to look at the widow. Her eyes were
wet with tears and her lip quivered but her head was up
and her chin set at a proud angle.

"Thank you," she said to the Gunsmith as if he were
the only man alive.

"You're welcome," he replied quietly. Then, looking
back at the crowd, he said, "You pay me great honor
here today, but what I'd really like to see is this town's
name changed from Santa Rosa to Evansville. Evansville in honor of the brave little man who sounded the
alarm and dashed so damned bravely into certain death.
What do you say folks?"

They said yes. They said it with shouts and cheers and
an applause that filled the street and then echoed out
into the Sangre de Cristo Mountains.

Clint was enjoying himself far more than he'd expected to. The Evansville idea had been a spur of the
moment idea, an inspiration worthy of the little shop-
keeper. Mary Evans and her children were all crying
now, but they were tears of joy. They had never expected to have their name so honored.

Even Milly was crying happily and old Ace was studying Clint with a smile. Their eyes met and then Ace did a
funny thing—he tipped his battered Stetson in salute.
Clint figured he was being accorded a real tribute by the
crusty cattle baron.

Clint reached over and grabbed the mayor's arm.
"Pound your gavel or whatever you do and proclaim

that this town is now and forever hereafter to be known as Evansville.''

The mayor seemed only too happy to oblige. And so, the act was done. Clint felt mighty good about knowing he had put little Dade's name on the map.

But there were three men who seemed detached and unmoved by his words. Rafe Longely, Jepson Hathaway and the thickly muscled blacksmith and part-time sheriff, Jerome. Clint looked deep into the eyes of all three and saw only malice. Their looks caused the wide grin on his face to evaporate.

Unconscious of the act, his hand moved closer to the butt of his gun. Just when he thought he'd done something real special, along came someone else to remind him that there were always jealous and mean sonsofbitches around who liked nothing better than to destroy a self-satisfied man.

NINE

Clint and Milly took the first dance while everyone watched. Milly's cheeks were flushed with happiness and she danced beautifully.

"I didn't know cowgirls could dance so well," Clint said teasingly.

"This cowgirl can," she told him. "Besides, I had no idea a gunfighter would know a waltz from a Virginia reel."

Clint smiled. "I guess it just goes to prove that this old world is full of surprises."

"I talked to Pa and he said he wants you to come and live at the ranch for awhile. I almost fell over with surprise, Clint. It was the last thing in the world I expected. He isn't a very hospitable man."

"I'd imagine not. Especially toward a younger fella who might be interested in his daughter."

"And you are interested, aren't you, Clint." It wasn't a question; she knew damn good and well he was. "Will you come and let me teach you how to be a cattleman and rancher?"

"How about I just learn to be a half-assed cowboy?"

When the music stopped, Rafe Longely poked Clint on the shoulder. "Say, hero, there's a rodeo goin' on out in the corral. I just bet ten dollars a fancy gunslick like you couldn't ride anything but a dog-tame horse.''

Clint knew the man was spoiling for trouble and he was about to give him all he wanted. But he'd be damned if he'd fall into a trap and let some bronc stomp him into the dirt. ''I got a bullet in the backside and no interest at all in riding some handpicked outlaw you want to bust me in half.''

Rafe smiled meanly. ''Figures. You're a dude who's nothing without a gun in his fist.''

Clint started to push Milly away but she clung to him and said, ''You get outa here, Rafe! I swear I'll tell my Pa on you!''

''Do that,'' he said. ''Ace needs me and he damn sure don't need this gunfighter hanging around the ranch-yard collecting dust.''

''I'll pull my own weight,'' Clint said.

''That, I got to see, Hero.''

Rafe swaggered away and Clint had a hard time getting his mind back onto more pleasant things.

''Don't mind him,'' Milly said as the next dance began. ''He's just trying to scare you off.''

''I know. But what he doesn't understand is that badgering me has just the opposite effect. Tell me I can't do something and that makes me all the more determined to prove I can.''

When the music ended, several young men came over to ask Milly to dance. She seemed about to decline, but Clint said, ''Go ahead.''

''I just want to dance with you,'' she whispered in his ear.

''Sorry, but my tail is aching and I need a beer for the pain,'' he said. ''I'll be back to claim you for the last dance.''

''And then what? Can we go down to the river?''

Clint took a deep breath. "Might be fun," he said as he winked and strolled off the floor.

Clint did not see the massive forearm as it shot out from between the buildings. It was late in the day and the gaps between the buildings along Main Street were deep in shadow where Jerome waited. Now, as his muscular forearm choked off Clint's breath, Jerome dragged the much lighter man back into the deserted alley.

Clint had been caught from behind and never had a chance. One minute he was walking along thinking of what a fine time he and Milly would have this evening and the next moment he was being strangled. He fought with all his ebbing strength. Clint knew instantly that Jerome was going to kill him and struggled almost helplessly in the grip of a far bigger and more powerful man.

Clint slammed his elbow into Jerome's gut again and again but it bounced off as if he'd punched an Indian's war drum. He even tried to smash his heel down on the blacksmith's toes but the man wore such heavy boots that it had no effect. Clint tried to yank his gun free but Jerome anticipated that and tore it from his holster and hurled it into the alley.

"I'm going to fix your goddamn fancy wagon," Jerome growled as his arm squeezed down with killing pressure. "They took away my sheriff's badge and they want to hire you full-time, you conniving bastard!"

Clint wanted to tell the man that he didn't want to be sheriff of Evansville. Not even part-time. And he damn sure didn't need to wear Jerome's precious badge. But talking was impossible. Clint felt the power in his arms and legs fading quickly away, like sand from between a man's spread fingers.

Jerome got him into the alley and shoved his face into a rain barrel and Clint knew the meaning of blind terror. He was going to be drowned! No one was going to help and he was now too weak to fight.

Clint did the only thing he could do. He held his breath and went limp hoping Jerome would think he had drowned before he really died.

Clint felt his eyes bulge and his brain seemed to swell. His lungs caught fire and a thin, watery-red haze spread across the back of his eyes.

And then, he lost consciousness.

TEN

Clint was awakened by the jarring of a buckboard as it rattled up a steep mountain road. He was lying on his back, his wounded buttock bouncing painfully against the hard wooden bed of the wagon. Maybe he'd never have awakened if it hadn't been for his bullet wound.

When his eyes popped open, he thought it was the darkest night he had ever known until he realized that he was covered by a pile of smelly old horseblankets. Clint took a deep breath and gathered his thoughts. His hand moved down his side to his six-gun but it was gone. He pushed the blankets up a little from his face so he could breathe better and then he twisted around onto his side and peeked out from under the blanket.

It was night and quite dark. There were no stars in the heavens and damn little moonlight. Rain was falling and it was cold. The wind moaned through pine trees and he could hear a waterfall close by and the roaring of a swift river.

Clint peered up to see Jerome's massive back. The man was wearing a slicker. Clint cussed because the slicker was pulled over Jerome's sidearm and that was going to make things a whole lot tougher.

The Gunsmith knew he was no physical match for Jerome. And, without a gun, he didn't stand much chance of escaping from the huge man who was obviously taking him out to be buried. Clint decided the wisest thing he could do would be to slip quietly off the wagon and then try to reach Evansville. Once armed, he'd hunt down this muscle-bound giant and cut him down to size.

Clint began to ease off the back of the wagon. First his feet, then his knees, then he sat up quickly and rolled forward. Trouble was, one of the planks was loose and it jumped up and then crashed back with a loud bang. Clint hit the road face down in the mud and was momentarily blinded.

Jerome yelled something that reflected his shock and dismay. Clint heard the screeching protest of the wooden brakes being applied hard on the buckboard's wheels. A moment later, gunfire flashed in the rainy night. Clint pulled himself out of the mud and stumbled into the trees feeling weak and disoriented. He felt pine needles and brush slapping his face and he ran blindly into a fallen tree and crashed right over it. A sharp-edged branch ripped into his thigh and his leg went numb.

Jerome was coming. The big man was shouting and swearing. Clint tried to stand and hobble but his feeble effort was endangering his life so he dropped flat behind the rotting tree and pushed in close to hide. He listened to Jerome crash through the forest. Then, just when Clint thought Jerome was about to reach the buckboard, the big man turned back.

He passed within ten feet of Clint and when he reached the wagon, he yelled, "Gunsmith, come on out! You can't get away. Ain't nobody within twenty miles of us. This is an old logging road. It's just you and me."

Clint thought about getting up and making a run for

it. He thought about that for perhaps ten seconds before dismissing the idea as sheer folly.

A panicked man would probably run in fear. He'd use all of his strength blindly fighting his way around in the night. By morning, he'd be exhausted and hopelessly lost. Then Jerome would come and find him. The end would be almost merciful.

Clint reached down and felt his wounded leg. He was hurt but not seriously. If he survived Jerome, the leg would turn purple but heal in a few days. Clint clawed wood out from the soft, rotten underbelly of the decaying tree until he was completely hidden.

I'll wait until first light and take my chances, he thought. And then see what happens.

It rained all the rest of that night and cleared just before daybreak. Clint had stayed reasonably warm and dry under the fallen tree and might have been comfortable except for the damned wood ants that occasionally took a bite out of him.

At first light, Clint heard Jerome calling his name again. The man seemed to be circling the wagon looking for tracks. And, Clint thought, they should be pretty obvious. The ground had been wet and muddy and Clint had not had the time to worry about covering his tracks.

Clint knew that he had to leave the fallen tree. When Jerome did find his muddy tracks, they would lead him right to this spot. Clint did not relish the idea of having the blacksmith riddle him with bullets while he lay half-buried under a tree. So he forced himself to his feet. He had to grind his teeth together to keep from crying out in pain because his deeply bruised leg had stiffened and did not want to respond.

"Gunsmith," Jerome bellowed. "I'm gonna find you!"

Then do it! Clint thought angrily. But you had better watch your back, because I may find you first.

Clint took a deep breath and studied the pale, shadowy forest all around him. He had no idea which direction was which so he turned and headed for the roaring river. He might just as readily have gone in any other direction, but he was thirsty and the sound of the river would drown out the sound of his own passing.

Jerome thought he was the hunter: Clint figured that, if he had any chance of getting through this day alive, he was going to have to turn that situation around. But first he had to find a place to ambush the big man. And to do that, he needed to put some distance between them.

ELEVEN

The river was wide and strong. Initially fed by hundreds of little streams, it gathered into a mighty body of water that boiled savagely down from the snow-clad mountains. Clint studied it carefully. He could not swim it and, unless there was a tall pine tree lying across it, there was no possibility of crossing. How far back was Jerome? A half mile? Less than that, probably.

So, he thought, looking back over his shoulder and expecting to see the giant burst out of the forest at any moment, this could be the end of the hunt. I must find a place that gives me some advantage. He studied the massive rocks that followed the river down the mountain. He knew he did not have much time remaining. Jerome was coming and Clint had left a clear trail for him to follow.

He hobbled painfully toward the nearest pile of boulders and was careful to leave clear footprints in the sand. He wanted Jerome to follow and thought that perhaps he could climb up on the top of some rocks and then drop down on the man, stunning him long enough to take his gun. But once Clint was into the boulders, he knew that Jerome would expect such a trap and have his gun up and ready.

I will have to think of something a little more clever than that, Clint thought.

A house-sized, bone-white boulder jutted up against a huge and dangerous whirlpool. Clint studied the rushing circle of water and knew he wanted no part of it. The vortex was a swirling vacuum that dropped far under the surface of the river. Even as Clint watched, a branch was sucked under and disappeared. But Clint had to go on. There was a narrow ledge around the great white rock and he took it with more than a little apprehension. The ledge was so narrow that Clint was forced to hug the rock with his chest and stomach and inch along sideways. It was not difficult, and not especially dangerous as long as he did not lose his nerve and try to hurry. Actually, the water appeared safe along the very edge of the white rock. The center of the whirlpool was a good thirty feet away. Even so, Clint moved with extraordinary care and when he had traversed the ledge, he breathed a deep sigh of relief. That relief, however, was immediately dispelled when he realized that he was now in a small cove of rocks, absolutely trapped in a dead end. There was simply no place to climb even if he were in top physical condition. Three more large rocks were packed together so tightly it seemed as if they must have been mortared in place. There wasn't even a handhold or crack to jam his fingers or toes into.

Clint fought down his anger and fear. He swung around and started back fast. He had committed a serious error of judgment. One that could cost him his life. If Jerome caught him here under the overhang of these rocks, there would be nowhere to run, nowhere to hide. And the monster whirlpool made a chilling, sucking sound that Clint tried unsuccessfully to ignore.

Hobbling painfully, trying not to think of what he had done, Clint reached the mountainous white rock and stepped out onto the ledge. Then, his worst fears came true. He heard a branch snap close by and knew that Jerome was just around the corner.

Clint swung about wildly, seeking some avenue of escape but knowing there was none. What a trap he had laid for himself! If he was shot here, his body would never be found. The animals would strip his bones and the snows of next winter would cover them. In spring, the first great torrents of icy water would fill this gorge and carry his ravaged bones down the desolate mountainside and scatter them onto the valleys below.

I could not have picked a better spot for the man to finish me off, Clint thought miserably. He backed off the ledge knowing he had only one possible hope. Sitting down, he yanked off his boots, then stripped off his coat and shirt. He stepped into the icy current and quickly hugged the white rock as he eased into deeper water. He could feel the very edge of the mighty whirlpool's gentle but insistent tugging. Clint eased forward, hearing the gulping, sucking sound of the water as if it were calling to him. He sank until only his eyes and the top of his head were above the surface of the pool. He clung to the rock knowing that the narrow ledge just inches from his fingers would occupy every bit of Jerome's attention and require the man to holster his six-gun.

Clint pulled himself in tight against the mossy underbelly of the white boulder. His toes found a purchase and he wedged his knees in between the underwater rocks to hold his place against the swirling tidepool. When he saw pebbles strike the water just around the corner of the rock, Clint expelled the air from his lungs and sank underwater to wait.

He held his breath and slowly counted to forty before he allowed himself to ease upward and break the surface of the river. When he saw the giant directly overhead with his massive chest flattened against the rock, Clint lunged upward from the whirlpool and grabbed both of the man's boottops. Jerome shouted but Clint jammed his own knees up against the rock and then threw his body back with the all the power he had remaining.

Jerome had nothing to grip. With a tremendous splash, he hit the river and the current gripped him like he was in the jaws of an alligator. His body began to circle, slowly at first, then faster as the mighty whirlpool swept him around and around.

"Help!" Jerome screamed in choking terror. "God, help me!"

"I don't even know if God could save you now," Clint said, almost feeling pity for the man as he gripped the edge of the rocks. He watched the giant being spun inexorably into the vortex of the whirlpool. The Gunsmith closed his eyes the moment Jerome was sucked underwater screaming.

Clint kept expecting to see Jerome's body come shooting back up to the surface somewhere downriver. But it didn't happen. The Gunsmith worked his way along the side of the white boulder until he could pull himself out of the water. He was shivering violently and almost blue with cold. But he was alive and Jerome was dead. And there was a horse and buckboard less than a mile away and a thick pile of horseblankets to crawl under until he warmed up.

Clint pulled on his shirt, his coat and his boots. His teeth were chattering together and his banged-up leg wasn't working quite properly. But he was alive. He'd done it all wrong and yet, it had turned out alright. Sometimes, Clint thought, as he started up through the rain-drenched forest, dumb or blind luck was better than brains.

Clint was hobbling pretty badly by the time he reached the buckboard but the hike up from the river had gotten his blood pumping strong. He didn't stop shaking until he had rubbed himself down with the horseblankets and started the team back down the mountainside.

Clint didn't really know what to tell anyone about Jerome, but sometimes it was better not to say anything at all. Jerome had a livery but no wife or kinfolk. His livery would probably be taken over by a better man and, as the months passed, people would just assume Jerome had run off for the same kinds of inexplicable reasons men have always walked away from things they once thought dear.

But Clint had a strong hunch that at least one man would know the truth of it. Rafe Longely and Jerome had been more than passing acquaintances; unless Clint had it judged wrong, he would bet anything the Hatha-way ranch foreman had put Jerome up to this murder-ing affair. Maybe he had gotten him drunk and teased him about losing his sheriff's badge until Jerome had been ready to kill.

But hell, Clint thought as he hurried the two horses along, I sure can't prove anything like that. Nope. Only me and Rafe will know the truth of the matter. And maybe young Jepson too, but I hope not.

TWELVE

Milly Hathaway tucked the covers under Clint's chin. "There," she said, proudly surveying her work, "I'll bet you've never been better taken care of in your life."

Clint just smiled. He had contracted pneumonia and been feverish for two weeks but now he was feeling pretty good. He knew that he was weak but he needed to work in order to get back into shape.

"I could have shaved myself, you know," he said.

"Of course I know," Milly responded. "But wasn't this more fun?"

Clint had to agree she had a point. Still, he was an active man and not one who enjoyed lying around for extended periods of time. On the other hand, he had gotten to know Ace Hathaway's daughter very well indeed and his regard for her had increased to the point where he thought he might even be falling in love with the girl. He liked having her close and he especially liked the way she crept into his bedroom late at night.

"How many children shall we have, Clint?"

He tried not to display his total lack of interest in such matters. "Well, if I ever have children . . . "

"You can't have them, but I might one of these days," she said with an impish wink.

"Yes," he said slowly. "I'm sure you could. Dammit,

61

Milly, I'm getting up and getting dressed. It's time I started paying my way around here."

There was a knock at the door followed by a loud, "I'm mighty glad to hear that, Gunslick."

Clint looked up and saw Ace filling the doorway.

The rough-hewn old rancher was hatless, his hair was white and he was covered with dust.

"Been out helpin' the boys break some green horses," he said. "That Rafe is almost as good a man on a horse as I used to be. You any kind of broncbuster a'tall?"

"Pa, that's not fair!"

"Quiet, girl. I jest asked the Gunslick a friendly question. Are ya?"

"Nope," Clint said. "I never break horses. Too rough on your body."

"Hmmm," Ace said, clearly not pleased by Clint's answer. "And yesterday, me and the boys roped and branded about a hundred calves up on the east side of the range. You ever swing a rope, Gunslick?"

"Gunsmith." It was starting to get on Clint's nerves a little the way the rancher kept fouling up his name. "Nope, I have lassoed a man off a horse. Once, I even tried to lasso a coyote but I got to swinging the rope so hard I lost control of the damned thing and it wrapped around my neck and I almost choked. So I leave roping to the real cowboys."

"Hmmm," Ace rumbled. "You really are a damned greenhorn sonofabitch, ain't ya."

"Pa, that's . . . "

"Quiet girl! I just thought I needed to know what this here fella can do."

Clint swung his legs out of bed and pulled on his pants and then his boots. "What I can do is walk and shoot straight. I can fight with my fists, but I'd rather settle an argument with words and reason than bones or bullets."

Clint grabbed his shirt, knowing that his ribs were showing and that he was too damned thin. "I'm not the kind of man you want for a son-in-law, Ace. And I probably ought to say you aren't the kind of man I'd choose for a father-in-law. Thing of it is, that's getting way ahead of ourselves. I haven't any idea yet of marrying your daughter."

"Hmmm! Well, you kissed her, ain't you!" he bawled, stomping into the room with his huge fists clenched at his sides.

He was very intimidating. Clint stood his ground though, and said, "Yeah, I kissed her plenty. And don't ask me such questions again. A gentleman don't talk about such things. You know that."

Ace wasn't used to facing a man as strong-willed as himself. "You're right," he finally drawled. "Excuse me, Milly darlin'. I was outa line there. But I am fixin' to round up some cattle outa the west end of my range tomorrow. Gunsmith, I was wondering if your sore ass was up to the ride."

"It is," Clint said. "But I'd like someone to go into town and ride back my gelding, Duke."

"He a cowhorse?"

"No."

"Then I don't want the sonofabitch on the spread," Ace said shortly. "A horse that don't savvy cows ain't worth feedin'."

"My horse is better than anything you have on this ranch," Clint told the man evenly. "If you won't have him, I leave."

"Pa!" Milly wailed. "Let him have his horse. They can learn cattle together."

The old man bristled and fumed. But with Milly looking up into his face as if she was begging for her very life, Ace crumpled soon enough. "Alright," he conceded. "But you made a pretty damn big brag there. Can that horse of yours do anything good?"

"He's fast and he doesn't get tired easy," Clint said, still ruffled by the man.

"We'll see," the rancher promised. "We'll just see how tough both you and him is. Ranchin' ain't easy like gunsmithin'. It's hard work."

"When you're a man with my reputation, Ace, just staying alive is hard work."

The rancher liked that. He almost grinned. "Tomorrow we ride out at sunrise. Your horse will be fed and saddled. It's up to you if you ride him or not. But nobody is goin' to baby you jest because you been sick and almost died. Same goes for the horse. Fact he ain't used to bein' rode all day don't mean spit on this ranch."

"I'll warn the horse," Clint said drily.

Ace nodded. "You best get to bed early tonight and sleep well." He emphasized the word "well" so that it left little doubt in anyone's mind that he was not completely ignorant of what was going on between the Gunsmith and his daughter. But still, if he ever realized the whole of the thing, Clint knew he was going to have more trouble than he knew what to do with.

Milly did not creep into Clint's room that night and the Gunsmith was just as glad. He slept soundly and awoke refreshed an hour before daylight when he heard the cook banging on his triangle to announce that breakfast was ready.

When Clint walked outside and crossed the ranch-yard, he took a deep breath of fresh air. It felt real good to be up and around. But when he walked into the cookshack and all the cowboys ignored him, the pleasure went right out of his day.

Clint grabbed a plate and shoved it before the cook. "I'm the skinniest man in here," he said roughly. "So fill it up."

The cook wasn't used to being ordered around that way and it showed. But one glance into Clint's eyes told him that the Gunsmith was not in the mood for an argument. He filled the plate and after Clint got a cup of coffee, he had to practically lever his way onto a bench so he could eat.

Rafe ignored him completely and it seemed to Clint that the other cowboys were probably just following Rafe's example because they were afraid not to. So, Clint thought, this is the way it is going to be.

He finished up his meal and then pitched his cup and plate into a bucket of hot, soapy water. Outside, the sky to the east was just starting to lighten up a little. Clint walked across the yard feeling only a small twinge of pain on his buttock. He was as ready as he was ever going to be for this day.

When he stepped into the corral and Duke nickered a greeting and stepped out from the other horses to be bridled, Clint really felt good. All the other cowboys had to rope their ponies and some of them even missed the first loop.

Clint warmed the bit in his hand and then bridled his horse. He said to the cowboy next to him, "A man who knows how to train his horse doesn't need to rope and then buck him out every danged morning."

The cowboy ground his teeth together and reshaped his catch loop. He didn't find Clint's comment a damn bit amusing.

But then, Clint hadn't expected him to.

THIRTEEN

They gave Clint a grass rope and he took it without
much comment. As a boy he had fooled around with the
things until he was really good at roping old dogs, too
stiff to move fast, along with such other things as sage-
brush, tortoises and little kids. He had never had any
success roping calves, goats, cats, chickens or young
dogs that could move quickly.

Ace rode in the lead with Rafe at one of his stirrups
and young Jepson at the other. Jepson, though a six-
footer, looked boyishly small in comparison to the other
two men. Hell, Clint thought, I'd look small too next to
either Ace or Rafe. They were both exceptional physical
specimens, tall and extraordinarily wide-shouldered.
Ace had thickened a little around the midriff where
Rafe was still lean, but other than that, they might have
been mistaken for father and son. But if there was little
physical difference between them, there was a vast dis-
parity in their characters. Both were hard, gruff men,
but Ace was known for his honesty and forthrightness.
A handshake was his bond and when he didn't like
something or somebody, he let it be known. Rafe, on
the other hand, was shifty. He had a cunning that made
him the more dangerous of the pair. Of the two, Clint
would much prefer to have Ace mad at him and know

he would not be ambushed or shot in the back.

These were Clint's thoughts as the men galloped out into the sunrise and headed for a distant range. The morning was crisp and cool, the horses peppery and ready to run. They set a brutally fast pace for the first seven or eight miles. Ace and his cowboys seemed to be trying to outdistance Clint and Duke but it soon became apparent that the black gelding was more than a match for anything they rode. In fact, Clint had to hold his horse in a little to keep the powerful gelding from turning it into a flat-out horse race.

They crossed two good-sized rivers that had no name and rode up a valley filled with grass and summer flowers. The day grew pleasant and by nine o'clock in the morning Clint guessed that they had already covered nearly fifteen miles. Ace split the cowboys between himself and Rafe.

"Clint," he said, "you ride with Rafe and his part of the crew this morning."

"Sure," Clint replied, seeing the flicker of a grin on some of the cowboy's faces.

"What we want to do is to comb the brush and canyons for unbranded cattle," Ace said. "Then, we drive them all down yonder by that big pole corral and brand 'em. Take us about ten days of brush-poppin' and brandin' to clear out this section of the ranch. Afterwards we'll move on to another section."

"Ten days?" Clint hadn't expected to stay for even one night. And Milly hadn't said anything about this. Clint was beginning to smell fish. He'd assumed that Rafe was going to try and make him look like a fool and a quitter, but Clint sure hadn't thought that Milly and Ace were going along with that plan.

"Maybe even longer, Gunsmith," Rafe said with obvious enjoyment. "What's the matter? You have something better to do?"

Clint pulled his new Stetson down tight on his forehead. "Not a single thing," he said.

"Good. Then come on and let's round-up some cattle."

Ace looked Clint dead in the eye. "Don't you go bustin' your fool neck, Gunsmith. Or that horse's leg, either."

"Not a chance," Clint replied as he touched spurs and set out after Rafe and his band of cowboys.

They rode far up into the steep mountainside and ravines and then Rafe ordered each of his men to take a different ravine and comb it of all livestock. It did not surprise Clint to learn he was being assigned the deepest and most brush-choked ravine of the lot.

"Alright," Rafe said, "we drive them on down and I don't want anyone to miss a single head. Let's ride!"

Clint noticed how all the other cowboys glanced at him as they untied their ropes. Clint left his rope tied to his saddle. To hell with trying to rope anything as big and fast as a cow, especially one running full tilt down a mountainside. He sent Duke ahead and moments later they were plunging down into the thick brush. The brush was higher than a man on horseback and covered with sharp spines that quickly scored Duke's silky coat and made long rents in Clint's pants.

A cow and her unbranded calf seemed to appear out of nowhere and Clint reined the big gelding after it. The cow tried to cut back up the draw but Duke was horse enough to swap ends and head it off in time. But the moment he had it turned, the cow saw a scree of rocks and shot across it with its calf right behind. Duke went after them and it seemed to Clint a miracle that the big horse was able to hold its footing on the loose rock. But finally, after a reckless ride of almost five minutes, the cow was played out and its calf was staggering with fatigue.

Clint was furious at the stupid cow that had caused him to risk Duke's legs and his own life. He cussed the contrary thing and when it responded by trying to bolt in the wrong direction, Clint quickly untied his rope and used the end of it to pop the fool cow across the muzzle—hard! The cow bawled in pain and, tail straight up, headed on down the ravine exactly where it was supposed to go.

That made Clint feel pretty good until he came on two more cows and their calves with exactly the same contrary frames of mind as the first one. Then he was faced with double-trouble. He'd drive Duke after one set and just when he had them turned, the other pair would bolt for freedom and have to be chased down all over again. Back and forth they raced in a mad scramble over brush, rocks and deadfall. It was almost a draw as to who ran out of steam first, Clint and Duke, or the cows and their calves.

But they were determined to clear the ravine and they did, though Duke was covered with foam and ringing wet with sweat by the time the two cows gave up. To his great relief, however, once he had six animals all going downhill, the other cows that Clint came across seemed inclined to join them. And two weary hours later, Clint had at least forty cows and their baby calves moving out into the valley. For a moment, he was feeling pretty good about things, and then he saw the other cowboys and they were each bringing about twice as many cattle down the mountain. And the worst part of it was that their horses were a lot fresher than poor Duke!

The Gunsmith clenched his teeth and dismounted. It was clear that he was at fault. There were always tricks to doing anything the easy, as opposed to the hard, way, and not a single man on this roundup was going to share them with Clint.

He loosened his cinch and then checked the gelding's forelegs and chest. There were some angry scratches and a little blood but no deep, scarring cuts. Still, Duke was trembling with fatigue, his head hung lower than Clint had ever seen it hang before.

"Hey!" Rafe yelled. "Get back on that horse and come drive these cows to the corral!"

Clint made a sign with his upraised fist that left no doubt that he did not intend to ride Duke another step until the gelding caught his wind and cooled down. Rafe's face grew dark with anger but he sent two of his cowboys to drive Clint's cows and calves in with the rest. Then they all trailed on toward the big corrals for the branding.

Clint waited almost half an hour. He was the only man on the crew not wearing heavy cowhide chaps and now his pants were shredded. Had it not been for his high boottops, he'd have been in a bad fix. Clint pulled off his Stetson and wiped his brow with his forearm as he watched the distant dustcloud recede.

"Well," he said to his tired horse, "we've been through worse fixes than being run to death by a few cows and calves. Might as well go and see what kind of fun a cowboy has at the old branding corral."

Duke nickered tiredly in reply. And when Clint got back in the saddle, he found he was already stiff and sore. If he survived this first day of the roundup, it was going to be hell getting his body out of his bedroll in the morning.

FOURTEEN

The first afternoon's gather must have totaled over three hundred cows and calves and the pole corral was straining to hold them all. Ace had the branding irons red-hot before he ordered his cowboys to start to work.

Clint walked up to the rancher. "What am I supposed to do?"

"You kin sit and watch."

"Uh-uh," Clint said stubbornly. "I want to learn this cowboying business so I can at least say I tried it once."

Ace held a cigarette with one hand and used the other to dig a match out of his front shirt pocket. "Alright," he drawled, "it's your funeral but I don't think you're up to it."

"Let me decide that."

"Watch these boys a minute before you put your foot in your mouth and choke to death on shoe leather."

At a signal from Ace, mounted cowboys rode into the corral and cut out a cow and her calf. A cowboy swung the gate open and when the cow and calf darted for the hills, Rafe shot out after them with his rope whirring in the wind. He swung it overhead so fast it was a blur, and it caught the darting calf by the neck. The little fella hit the end of the rope and flipped over backward.

Its mother reversed direction and Clint thought that she was going to come charging back, but she stopped and bawled pathetically as two cowboys raced on foot to the calf. One grabbed its heels and stretched it out against the taut rope while the other slapped a cherry-red branding iron against its shoulder. Acrid smelling grey smoke rose thick and choking. The calf thrashed and bawled. The man pitched his branding iron toward the fire then grabbed his pocket knife.

With quick slashes, he notched the calf's ear and then he castrated the poor little critter. The entire procedure took less than two minutes but, while it lasted, there was a lot of blood and dust. Rafe spurred his horse forward and the rope went slack. It was removed and then Rafe coiled it quickly and another cow and calf were cut from the herd and came flying through the gate. The entire procedure was repeated, only faster this time.

Several other ropers took positions outside the corral as the cowboys grouped into three-man teams. Ace watched a minute then frowned disapprovingly. "They'll get it down to less than a minute by the time it gets dark. They always start slow."

"That's slow?" Clint could not believe his ears. The cowboys had worked like a well-oiled machine.

"Yep," Ace replied. He glanced at the Gunsmith. "Now, which job did you figure you're qualified to do?"

Clint shrugged his shoulders. "I could do the gate man's job."

"I dunno," Ace said slowly. "Sometimes you hafta throw yourself in front of a cow or a calf if more'n one was to charge the gate all together. Otherwise, we could have a stampede out there and them sonsofbitches will scatter like leaves in a cyclone. Be dark before we could get them all back in the corral. Lose lotta time that way."

"I think I can do it," Clint said with determination.

"Okay," the rancher said after a moment, "but if they stampede, you have to turn every damn one of 'em before they get through."

Clint stepped out of the saddle, tied Duke to the corral and went to the gate man. He took his place but he could see the cowboy wasn't very happy about being replaced.

The first half-dozen or so cows came flying out with their calves in pairs just like they were supposed to. But then, for no reason that Clint could see, four cows all decided they wanted to be free at the same time. One minute Clint was standing by the gate feeling he was doing a pretty fair job of cowboying, and the next instant about a ton of beef was thundering toward him.

He snatched off his Stetson, jumped into their path and waved his arms. "Yaaah!" he screamed. "Yaaaahhhhhh!" The first wild-eyed cow hit him right in the chest with its stubby little horns and flattened him. The other three cows ran right over his chest. Clint dimly felt the little calves dance across his body as the other cows, seizing the opportunity, charged.

Ace Hathaway was the only man who cared enough to reach Clint in time to save his life. He grabbed the Gunsmith by the arm and jerked him out of the gateway just as the other cattle came pouring in like a river through a broken floodgate.

Ace swore a blue streak and then he was hurrying for his mount. One minute everything was a well-run performance of men, horses and cattle, the next minute it was total chaos as the entire herd broke for freedom.

Clint dragged himself up the fence. He watched the bunch of them thundering off. When they were all gone and things got quiet, Clint hobbled over to Duke feeling every step of the way as if he was going to die.

Duke nuzzled him softly. Clint stroked the horse's

sweat-caked neck and brushed the dirt and cowshit from his own clothes. "Old friend," he said to the horse, "if it wasn't for the fact that they all expected you and me to quit, I'd sure ride outa here and never look back. But that would leave Milly with nothing but Rafe and a lifetime of bad news. We gotta stay put and stick it out, Duke. You can understand that, can't you?"

The weary horse bobbed his head to the filthy, beaten man who owned him. Man and horse, they needed to stick together when the going got rough.

A week later, Clint began to get the hang of hazing cows and calves out of the heavy brush. Or maybe Duke got the hang of it. That was probably closer to the mark because Clint started to let the reins fall loose and allow Duke to be a cowhorse. At any rate, they seemed to start anticipating the places where livestock liked to hide and then they anticipated the direction in which the cow would sprint. Clint wasn't sure exactly what they began to do differently, but it was working.

Not that he measured up to the other cowboys. They had a sixth sense about cattle that had taken years to refine. But Clint no longer felt angry or ashamed by the number of cattle he was rounding up. Besides, Rafe continued to give him the worse ravines, the most dangerous arroyos and hillsides to scour.

Clint discovered he was doing a whole lot better at the branding corral too. No more gate-guarding, though. Instead, he became the man who grabbed the calf's hind legs and stretched them out to be branded and castrated if necessary. He was amazed at how strong a calf really was. Some of them threw him all over the place but he hung on and began to get better and better until he did not believe he slowed anyone down.

"Why don't you try the branding, ear notchin' and

castratin'," Ace said one long afternoon. "Only way you'll learn is by tryin' it."

"You can learn by watching," Clint said. "Besides, I don't have a knife."

"You kin use mine."

"No thanks."

Ace shook his head. "That plumb disappoints me, Gunslick."

"Give me your damn knife."

Clint took it and did the job as required, but he didn't like it one bit. It was grim, bloody work that had to be done. He felt sorry for the calf but that didn't stop him from slicing its scrotum and then yanking the testicles out of their sack and cutting them away cleanly. He did it all one afternoon and the next day he gave Ace back his knife. Nothing more was ever said about it. But Ace went back to calling him Gunsmith again.

At the end of the tenth day, as predicted, they were finished and rode back to ranch headquarters. Milly was waiting on the porch and when she saw Clint and Duke, how they were still sitting upright though bloody and rough-looking, she let out a small whoop of happiness and came racing across the yard.

When Clint saw her so pretty and happy, he just forgot everything but the girl. He dismounted and took Milly into his arms, gave her a twirl in the air and then kissed her hard.

Milly looked up into his face. "You look awful," she confessed. "But you did it! You stuck."

"Yeah, I stuck. So did Duke."

"I knew you would. I swore to Pa I'd stay away for ten whole days if he promised not to let you get killed."

Clint looked over at the cowboys and the rancher. Now, he understood. It had all been a test and he had, somehow, passed that test. Milly was his reward.

Rafe bent over and spat into the dust. He glared at Clint and said, "A hand has to break his own string of horses. Tomorrow, we start."

Clint nodded. He was not a horsebreaker but he sure knew a lot more about them than he had cows and calves. "I'll be ready," he promised.

"We'll see about that."

Clint felt his spirits sag a little. How many times did he have to prove to these men that he wasn't a quitter? How many times was he going to have to have his body abused and smashed until one of the stone-faced cowboys who rode on Ace's payroll smiled or said a single kind, encouraging word?

Clint did not know. But with Milly so happy and the thought of her coming to see him tonight, he figured it was going to be all right.

"By the way," Ace rumbled, "when ya came, ya was a sick guest. Now, you're on the payroll and that means you bunk in the bunkhouse with all the other boys. Savvy?"

Clint hid his disappointment well. "I savvy."

"Then go put your horse away. Give him some feed along with the others. He ain't much, but I guess he's earned a bit of oats."

"Yeah," Clint said, "I guess he has at that."

"But Pa!" Milly wailed.

"Leave him go with the boys," Ace said. "Tomorrow, he's gonna have enough ridin' to do for a long, long time."

Clint turned toward the corral. He sure didn't like the sound of things to come.

FIFTEEN

The bunkhouse was silent as a tomb that night and the cowboys, being so tuckered out after ten days of roundup, went straight to bed. The trouble was, Clint did not see an empty bunk except for the one with a bunch of gear piled on top of it.

Clint studied the situation, hoping that someone would offer to clear the busted saddle and bridles away, but when no one offered, he figured they weren't leaving him any choice but to do it himself.

He was bone weary and in a foul mood. He had anticipated a nice dinner with Milly and Ace, then a return to his former private bedroom and finally, around midnight, Milly Hathaway in his arms once again. Clint thought he deserved a bath, too. Instead, he ate the cook's greasy stew, washed under the pump using a common, dirty towel, and now he was standing in this crowded bunkhouse with not even a lousy straw mattress to bed down on.

The hell with them, Clint thought. I've tried to earn their respect. All they've given me is their ice-cold silence. Without a second thought, Clint gathered up the whole pile of gear and threw it on the bunkhouse floor.

"Pick it up," a sharp-faced cowboy by the name of Laramie said. "Some of that is mine."

Clint looked over at the man. They were about the same height but Laramie was a good twenty pounds heavier. Clint glanced over at Rafe, who was smiling. "I see the lay of things now," Clint said. "First I gotta whip Laramie, then I gotta whip you."

Rafe shrugged inoffensively. "The saddle you dumped on the floor belongs to Laramie, it sure ain't mine."

"Pick it up, brush it off and set it right back where it was, along with that other stuff," Laramie said belligerently.

Clint sighed. "Okay," he said softly. He bent down, picked it up and, just as Laramie started to smile with smug triumph, Clint slung the saddle and almost took the man's leering face off. Laramie crashed into the wall, his face momentarily dull with shock and pain. Then he cussed a long streak and sleeved his bloody nose.

"Get him, Laramie!" a cowboy growled. "Bust his ass."

Laramie came off the wall swinging. He was young, fast and tough. Clint ducked a punch, took a second one and then delivered his own sweeping uppercut to the midsection. It landed hard enough to raise Laramie off the floor and when his boots came down, Clint smashed him in the nose again. The man tripped over a bunk and would have fallen if someone had not caught him.

"Get up and go after him," a cowboy said, shoving Laramie forward at Clint. "Hit him back. You can take him!"

Laramie wasn't so sure anymore. For that matter, neither was Clint when the man came in swinging again. They exchanged hard punches and Clint, being the lighter one, backed up a few inches. The cowboys saw this and began to cheer for their friend to "finish the dude off!"

That made Clint even madder. His blows whistled and he delivered two solid overhands that rocked Laramie back on his heels. But Clint was taking hard punishment and his face was numb. He ducked a windmill right and slammed a fist to Laramie's solar plexus. The man gasped and Clint jabbed him in the eye and then opened up his right cheek with a thundering punch.

Laramie went down and did not even try to get up. The Hathaway Ranch cowboys stared at their comrade and it was a moment before it seemed to sink in that Laramie had been soundly whipped. Then they seemed to close in toward the Gunsmith but it was Rafe whose cutting words stopped them in their tracks.

"That bridle and those reins on the floor belong to me. Pick them up, Gunsmith. A greenhorn on this ranch sleeps on the floor or in the dirt outside. Don't matter to me which one."

Clint's ears were ringing and he could feel one of his eyes swelling shut. He'd beaten Laramie fairly but it had cost him some damage. Now he was supposed to fight a man who was a half-foot taller and fifty pounds heavier. He balled his swollen, bruised knuckles and said, "There's some left for you, Rafe, so come and get it."

Rafe grinned broadly. "It's about time," he said. "I waited too long already."

The bunkhouse door slammed open. "Hold it!" Ace roared.

Everyone in the bunkhouse turned to see the big rancher who watched Laramie try to get up off the floor. Ace also took a good look at Clint's face and hands. He glanced up at Rafe and said, "This ain't right, nor fair. Not by a damn sight it ain't."

Rafe shouted in anger, "I'm the foreman and I'm in charge of these men."

Ace squinted, his massive shoulders hunched forward aggressively. "That can be changed damn quick and it just might be tonight, Rafe. You and all the rest of the boys have been testin' the Gunsmith every minute of every day. And he's passed every test with grit and hard tryin'. Now, this is goin' too damn far. Clint, you come on up to the house and take a room."

But Clint shook his head. "I just claimed a bunk and I want no special favors."

Ace seemed to like that reply. He nodded but before he turned away he unbuckled the gun and holster on his hip and said, "Milly says you lost your gun somewheres before you came here. That gun shoots a hair low. I figure a gunsmith like you could fix it real easy."

He pitched Clint the gun and holster. It was a beautiful set and the leather work was a piece of artistry. Clint glanced at the gun and nodded his thanks. He had lost his pistol when Jerome had caught him in the alley and almost choked him to death. He had another in his bedroll and he had also taken the precaution of wearing a derringer. But this was a real fine weapon, almost the equal of the one he had lost.

"I might not be able to get around to adjusting the sight and balance right away," Clint said, balancing the Colt Peacemaker and liking the feel of it.

"Ain't no hurry, Gunsmith. You wear it awhile and see what you think. Anything goes wrong around here, you have my permission to try it out just as fast as you want."

"I'll do that," Clint said, rolling his bedroll across the mattress. He smiled and, just before Ace stepped outside, he said, "tell Milly good night for me, Ace."

Rafe went purple with rage. He shot out the door after Ace and Clint listened to hot, angry words trail all the way to the house. He took his gun and walked outside just in case there was any real trouble. But when Ace slammed the door in Rafe's face and the lights of the ranch house went out, Clint went back inside and stretched out on his bunk.

He was dead tired and his face felt like it had been mule-kicked. But he'd whipped Laramie and he'd earned Ace's support. And had he even seen a smile on the face of some of the better cowboys when he'd asked Ace to tell Milly good night? Maybe. It had been a foolishly given barb but he was glad he'd used it anyway.

Now, if he could just survive tonight's treachery and then tomorrow's broncbusting, he had a feeling he would have everything under control.

SIXTEEN

All the corrals were full of wild broncs and, by noon, each cowboy had been assigned an even half dozen to ride. The idea was to ride them to a standstill for five straight days and then they were considered broke. There was no time for gentleness or even a hint of patience. These horses were broncs and Ace had bought them from mustangers out of the southeast part of New Mexico. They weren't pretty and some of them were seven or eight years old, long past the time when it was normal to break a horse to ride.

Dust churned, flies droned and cowboys cussed as Rafe shouted out names and horses and each cowboy claimed his own until only six remained, the worse half dozen of the entire band.

"What's left is your string of horses," Rafe said tightly. "You ride 'em every one, or you ride out."

Clint studied the six animals with no small amount of apprehension. He had never seen such a collection of misfits and jugheads in his entire life. There was a roan gelding with feet the size of dinner plates and a head shaped like a keg of nails. The sorrel was clearly a man-killer and the black had a look in its eye that left no doubt it meant to stomp, bite or kick anything that came within striking distance. The bay horse they'd chosen for him was still a stallion and the only one that looked as if it had any sense at all was an Appaloosa, but Clint knew that breed was notorious for hard bucking.

"Which one you gonna start to break?" Jepson asked as he strolled over from the ranch house. He looked dissipated and Clint had not seen much of him the last week. It was said that Jepson did nothing as well as he drank and chased fast women; Clint could see that he had been doing more than his share of both.

"Tell you the truth, they all look like outlaws or worse, but I guess I'll start with the Appaloosa," Clint decided out loud.

Jepson smiled and said, "That's the one we thought you'd pick. I could ride her to a halt, Gunsmith, but you never will."

"Shut up!" Rafe said harshly. "Just have someone lay a loop on the damn thing and let's see the hero ride." He was in a vile mood and dangerously close to snapping. Clint guessed that, after last night's argument with Ace, it was only a matter of time until his temper and his mouth got him fired.

Clint walked away from the man and grabbed his saddle. Two cowboys on horseback cut the Appaloosa out from the rest. One roped the forelegs and the horse spilled hard; the exploding air from its lungs made a loud "whooshing" sound. The other man jumped to the ground and blindfolded the Appaloosa without getting bit even once. He then hobbled the animal's front forelegs and, when the mare stormed to its feet, it tripped and crashed down again. This time, Clint was moving into the corral. He knew that indecision could play no part of what was to follow. He slung his saddle over the horse as it tried to bite him. Clint tightened the cinch while a halter and rope were applied. He caught a glimpse of Milly and her father standing by the corral. Milly looked worried. "Try and keep his head up!" she shouted.

Clint nodded. He might not be a broncbuster but he had been riding horses all his life. Yet, when he put his foot in the stirrup and swung his leg over the cantle he was not prepared for the eruption that nearly shot him into the sky. The Appaloosa went straight up and came straight down on stiff legs. The cowboys called it "pile-drivin' a man" and the description fit. Clint felt his backbone almost break and when the horse shot up into the sky again, his neck snapped back so hard he momentarily lost consciousness.

When he awoke a few seconds later, he was being unwrapped from the top rail of the pole corral and Rafe was grinning from ear to ear. Clint shook his head trying to clear his vision. He knew he had to get back on that horse.

"Jepson, no!" Ace roared.

When Clint staggered around, he saw the young man vaulting into the saddle. Jepson whooped, grabbed his Stetson and used it to fan the Appaloosa who just went crazy. Even so, Jepson rode the thing like it was a rocking horse. That Appaloosa tried every dirty trick it knew and a few it made up but Jepson never once appeared in danger of getting pitched. And when the ride was over, the Appaloosa was thoroughly beaten.

Jepson hopped off and led the exhausted animal over to Clint. "The others will be easier," he promised, "but I still don't know if you're rider enough to break one of them."

It was one of the most arrogant, conceited displays Clint had ever seen and it so completely disgusted Ace

Hathaway that he spat with contempt before walking away. "If you jest worked at it, goddammit, you could be the best! But you won't even half try!"

Jepson, stung by his father's outburst, whirled away and went off to ride his own string of horses. Rafe looked furious as he stalked off in the young man's wake.

Milly just shook her head. "Clint, do you know why he did that?"

"No."

"He had to prove himself better than you at something. Anything. He really admires you."

"I admire the way he rides. I never seen anyone better."

"He used to want to be a broncbuster," Milly said, watching her brother. "That's all he cared about— horses. But Pa wouldn't let him ride the broncs except when he had to. Pa is crippled up and he didn't want Jepson to be like him, stiff and hurting all the time. But it drove a wedge between them so deep it will never be forgotten. Jepson gave up and turned to whiskey and women. Clint?"

"What?"

"I don't want you to have to ride the rest of those horses. He gave you the worst of the bunch even after Rafe promised me he wouldn't do this to you."

"He promised you that?"

"Yes."

"Why?" Clint demanded.

"In return for . . . " She could not look him in the eye. "For a kiss," she said quickly as she started to hurry away.

Clint grabbed her by the arm. "Don't ever make another promise to that man," he said in a firm but gentle voice. "Not for me or for anyone."

She nodded, reached up and touched his cheek and studied his black eye. "Did he do that to you last night?"

"No, Laramie did."

She brightened. "No wonder I didn't see him this morning. He probably looks even worse than you."

"He does for a fact," Clint said. "Now, I better get back and try those other horses. Which one do you think is the worst?"

"The black."

Clint pointed it out to a couple of cowboys and they went in to rope it. It was Clint's experience in life that he was best off to go right after the toughest job and leave the easier ones for later.

One of the cowboys made the mistake of getting too close to the black's hind feet and it kicked his horse. The other managed to get his rope on the forelegs and bring the animal down but it was a squealing, harrowing moment before they could blindfold the animal and then get it hitched to the snubbing post.

The Gunsmith took a deep breath. "Have my epitaph read: Poor Clint Adams should have stuck to outlaw men instead of outlaw horses."

She kissed his cheek. "You can ride him," she cried out. "I know you can!"

Clint saddled quickly and mounted as the black launched into a wicked series of bucks that finally dislodged him and sent him somersaulting head over heels.

"You got him breathing hard!" Milly shouted. "A couple more times like that and he'll be finished."

Clint nodded and picked his aching body off the ground. Many of the cowboys had left their own horses for a minute to come and watch him. A couple even said a few encouraging words. Somewhere close by a big cloud of dust was rising up and being blown across the yard as another cowboy fought his bronc to a standstill.

Clint waited until the black was snubbed up tight again and then he jumped back into the saddle and yelled, "Turn him loose!"

The black reared up and crashed over backward. Clint just had time to kick out of the stirrup and throw his body sideways before he would have been crushed under the wild horse's weight. The black had stunned itself on impact and Clint had plenty of time to step into the saddle as the horse rose shakily to its feet.

He spurred hard and the black fought with renewed intensity. Clint hung on with his legs, his spurs and his hands. He grabbed onto the mane and saddlehorn and somehow, he stuck. And when the black finally gave up, Clint made it trot around and around the corral while the cowboys hanging off the trails grinned and congratulated him. It was one of the best feelings he had ever known.

Finally, he had won his spurs as a cowboy.

Milly was clapping her hands with excitement and even old Ace looked as happy as could be. "You'll make a hand yet, by gawd, maybe even a ramrod on this outfit!"

Clint smiled until he saw Rafe. The look on the Texan's face was pure poison. Clint knew that the man was finished messing around. No more getting men like Jerome drunk and in a killing rage and no more expecting a fella like Laramie to do his dirty work.

No, Clint thought, Rafe Longely is coming after me and it's going to be pretty damn quick.

SEVENTEEN

Jepson Hathaway's lean, hard young body was covered with a sheen of perspiration and his eyes were half-closed and glazed with whiskey and pleasure. He looked down at the face of the young whore he was screwing and she seemed almost young and innocently beautiful, though the last remnants of his senses told him she was not.

Her name was Cherry, and she was seventeen years old going on thirty-five. Her eyelids were puffy and closed, her lips slightly parted as her tongue darted in and out of her mouth like that of a snake. Cherry was plump, with small, pert breasts and thick, powerful thighs. She gripped Jepson between them and milked him energetically.

"Come on baby," she whispered urgently, "you can do it. I know you can!"

Jepson was trying for all he was worth. He'd been trying for almost fifteen minutes without success but so far . . . so far he just couldn't get past a certain threshold necessary to come in a jerking climax.

Cherry's eyes fluttered open. Like Jepson's, they were also glazed and bloodshot. Her slick, white body made wet, sucking sounds against his as they moved up and down on each other. She had already reached a climax twice and was inching her way toward another but she was physically exhausted and desperate to make him come. She liked Jepson very much but when he had been drinking too much, he just couldn't be a man this way. He ought to know that by now but she was just as stupid for taking his money and giving him a try.

"How's it feel?" she whispered, pumping hard and kneading his buttocks with her fingernails, then reaching over and between his legs to fondle his sack. He didn't even feel completely hard inside of her. "Are you coming, baby?"

"Yeah," he groaned, "I'm coming. Don't stop."

The fondling excited her more than it did Jepson. "Oh shit," she whispered, "here I go a . . . again!"

Her short, powerful legs shot out sideways and her strong, compact body shuddered violently. Cherry bit her lips and let herself rise up and crash down in a frenzy of ecstasy that left her feeling weak, spent and only a little furious at herself. The thing of it was, whores weren't supposed to do this and she would never have told the other girls but she loved to screw. Sometimes, she almost hated to take money for it. But Jepson had a lot of money, he always did. And he paid well, but not if he didn't come.

Cherry didn't have the strength to pump him anymore so she rolled him off of her.

"Hey," he muttered, "I was almost ready."

She didn't believe him because he was already limp. Besides, every man that Cherry had ever screwed to a dry standstill had said those very same words. "Sure honey."

She moved down his stomach and took his flaccid manhood in her mouth and began to fondle him with her teeth and tongue. In just a few moments he came alive and finally began to show real interest. Cherry soon had him writhing on the bed until he exploded, spewing his seed into her mouth. Cherry swallowed it automatically and then got up to rinse her mouth out with whiskey so that she wouldn't get a mouth infection. She gargled, spit the clouded whiskey into a bowl and drank two clean, deep swallows.

Jepson staggered to his feet and came over to take his bottle. "I ain't filled with no poison," he mumbled, obviously a little offended. "Here, Cherry honey. You sure earned it this time." He gave her ten dollars when most men gave her two or three. Jepson planted a wet kiss on her cheek and started to pull on his boots.

Cherry smiled. Jepson was a good boy. She thought of him as much younger than herself though she knew perfectly well he was several years older. "Jep," she said with a laugh, "I think you forgot something. Like puttin' on your pants first?" She lifted his pants, deftly slipping another five dollars out of the pocket because she had really earned it.

He giggled drunkenly. "Oh yeah!" With a slow-motion wink, he reached for her and they fell back on the bed laughing.

"Why don't ya stay with me, Jep? You're too drunk to ride all the way back to the ranch tonight."

"Gotta get back," he mumbled. "Big bad palomino sonofabitch to break in the morning. Ain't nobody else can ride him. Say he's a killer. Even Pa says he is. I'll show 'em all, though. Horse ain't no killer. He jess ain't met the right man yet."

Cherry shook her head. "When you gonna stop trying to prove you're the best broncbuster in New Mexico?"

"In the goddamn world!" he shouted.

"Okay," she said, helping him off with the boot he'd put on and then pulling him to his feet and raising one leg to poke through into his pants. "The world, then. I just think you oughta realize some time that your father, he don't give a damn about you, Jep. He really don't."

Jepson choked back a sob and swung at her but he missed and fell. He hadn't wanted to hit her anyway. Cherry was a good whore. He liked her a lot.

"Come on, Jep," Cherry said, pulling him back to his feet and helping him get dressed. "You know it's the truth. Your Pa plays favorites. He loves Milly, he just don't give a damn for you."

"Shut up and help me outa here," Jepson said, trying to sound mad but failing to. When she talked like this he really wanted to leave in a hurry but he was not sure if he could find the door, much less negotiate the stairs and locate his horse. "Cherry, you know what?"

"What?"

"You talk way too much for a whore."

"You should marry me, Jep. I'd stand up to Ace. I'd tell him straight to his face that you're a lot better man than he thinks you are."

"He thinks I'm horseshit," Jepson said with a catch in his throat. "And he'd think you were shit too, Cherry. He'd knock your ass off and then he'd kick mine all the way to Canada."

"I think you'd be better off hating 'em than the way you feel now. I don't understand why you don't tell the big bastard to go straight to hell. Leave the ranch and ride away."

He let her help him to the door. "Yeah, then whatta I got? Nothin'! Nothin' but a hangover and no money."

"You could get a job anywhere busting broncs. You

told me you were the best and I heard it from some other men, too. It's not just brag."

Jepson swelled with pride. "What other guys told you I was the best?"

"I can't remember. They all say it." She unlocked her door. "Stay the night and sleep it off, Jep. You can ride the palomino tomorrow afternoon instead of tonight."

"Uh-uh," he grunted. "Jest help me find my horse, Cherry. Do that and I'll give you my last five dollars."

"I already took it."

"Whore!" he raged feebly.

"Yeah, but you could make me a respectable woman, Jep. We could get married and face your Pa or even go away."

His handsome face screwed up. "Naw, that'd be a bad idea. Every guy in town's screwed you. You're a whore and you'll never be respec'able, Cherry."

Cherry swallowed painfully and said nothing as she helped him down the back stairs. She did this because she didn't want everyone to see Jepson Hathaway so drunk every night he came to town. And she did it because Jepson had stopped visiting the other saloon girls and whores and that meant he must care for her at least a little. She led him into the alley and then around the front to his horse.

"Goddamn," he whispered, kissing the animal on the muzzle. "Ya waited on me again!"

"Just like I do," Cherry said. "Comin' back tomorrow night?"

"You gonna do that again to me? You know, what you finally had to do to make me go?"

"If I have to, yes."

He crawled into the saddle and tipped his hat to her.

"You might have to, Cherry. I jest don't know anymore. Good-bye."

"No," she said, touching the rowels of the big Mexican spurs he loved to jangle when he walked, "it's just good night."

Jepson nodded and rode down the street without a backward glance. Cherry pulled her wrapper around her small, but firm little breasts and walked back toward the alley. He had left her some whiskey and she needed a few more drinks before she could go to sleep.

At the intersection of the alley, she turned and watched Jepson whip off his Stetson and smack his horse across the rump. The animal shot out of town and Cherry heard Jepson howl at the full moon.

Sometimes, she thought wistfully, I do think I love that boy and I sure wish he'd grow up and marry me. And I don't care what would happen, I'd still tell Ace Hathaway right to his face he was a big fool to treat his only son so damn bad.

EIGHTEEN

Jepson was chilled by the time he got to the ranch. There was a bottle of whiskey hidden in the barn near where the men kept their saddles. A drink would do him fine and warm him up good and proper.

He glanced at the ranch house and thought again about the Gunsmith. The man was all right. He'd proven he had a lot of sand and wasn't a quitter. Maybe, Jepson thought, I should be nicer to him. Especially if he marries Milly. From the way Ace was acting, that was almost assured. Ace had never treated anyone interested in Milly so nice. Probably, Jepson thought, as he dismounted and led his horse to the barn door, Ace wished he had a son like Clint Adams instead of one like me.

He pulled open the door and was surprised to see that the interior was bathed in soft lamplight. He was even more surprised to see Rafe bent over the Gunsmith's saddle with a knife in his hand.

"What the hell are you doin'?" he demanded.

"Shut up and close the door behind you!" Rafe ordered, his voice like a whipsting.

Jepson did as he was told. Then he led his horse over and watched as Rafe finished cutting the stirrup leathers so that they would break during a particularly rough ride.

Jepson's face screwed up with disapproval. "Hey," he said, "the man could get killed or at least busted up in the breakin' corral."

"I know. That's the idea."

"Now wait a damn minute," Jepson blustered, glancing over toward where his bottle ought to be.

Rafe was on his feet. He grabbed Jepson by the shirt-front and slapped him hard, once, then again. Jepson tried to struggle, but he was helpless and would have been so even if he was sober. "Let go a'me!" he whined.

Rafe threw him away like a piece of garbage. "Get your bottle and listen to me good," he said. "If the Gunsmith marries Milly, we both stand to lose everything. You're such a wreck that Ace is about ready to cut you out of the picture entirely. And me, I'll have worked like a dog to build this place up and I won't have Ace hand me my walking papers without so much as a word of thanks. And it could all happen because of the goddamn Gunsmith!"

Jepson shook his head and then he found his bottle. He hadn't thought much about it, but he supposed Rafe was right. "So what do we do?" he asked, taking a swig of whiskey.

"You don't do nothin'!" Rafe said, stabbing the knifeblade toward the Gunsmith's saddle. "I just took care of it. Milly won't marry a dead man or one that's too busted up to make her feel like a woman. And if a bronc don't do it tomorrow, I'll come up with something even better."

"You're a cunning sonofabitch," Jepson said, with a bad taste in his mouth. "I just wish there was some better way. I don't want to see him get hurt like that. Maybe if I just talked to him, explained things."

Rafe took a menacing step forward that sent Jepson backpeddling up to the wall. "Don't you touch me again, Rafe!" he cried. "So help me I won't stand for it anymore."

His hand dropped down to his gunbutt. When sober he was fast, but now Rafe simply looked at him with disgust.

"All right," he said, "I won't hit you. But sober up. You got a big ride tomorrow. If you're drunk, that palomino will stomp you flat as a pancake."

Jepson relaxed. "No he won't. I know how to ride him."

"We'll see," Rafe taunted. "A lot of the boys are saying you can't ride a woman anymore, much less a damned outlaw horse."

Jepson's cheeks colored and he shook with anger.

"Sometimes," he whispered.

Rafe waited. "Sometimes what, kid?"

Jepson's nerve failed him and he took a shuddering gulp of whiskey. "Never mind. I just want to go to bed."

"Do that," Rafe said. "I'll take care of your horse. You look like you been rode hard and put away wet. Go to bed."

Jepson nodded. He took one unsteady step and then another until he reached the barn door. "Grain him, Rafe. And rub him down a little, okay?"

Rafe said nothing, but the look in his eyes caused Jepson to shut the door and hurry on to the ranch house.

NINETEEN

When Clint arose the next morning, he heard two of the cowboys arguing about Jepson and the palomino stallion he was supposed to ride.

"Why," one of the cowboys said, "that sorry sonofabitch didn't even get to bed until three o'clock this morning! I saw him weavin' across the ranchyard as drunk as a damn skunk!"

"Drunk or sober," the other cowboy said, "Jepson is a natural bronc rider. The best I ever saw. If he ever started givin' a damn about hisself again, he could ride a hurricane. No siree, I figure that boy can ride the palomino to a standstill no matter what."

"Then I'll take your five dollars and raise you two more."

"Seven all together?"

"Yep."

"Hmmm. Okay, Smitty. I'll match your seven dollars and raise it an even three more."

"Ten dollars all together!"

"Yep."

"Sonofabitch! Oh, all right, Smitty. But you're gonna be techy as a teased snake all next month after you lose."

"I ain't gonna lose. Jepson can ride the horse."

Clint rolled out of bed and knuckled the sleep from his eyes. "When does he ride?"

"As soon as the old man can boot his ass outa bed and get him movin', I suspect. If you'd seen Jepson like I did last night, you'd know he was in pain this mornin'."

"Maybe he ought to wait and ride the palomino tomorrow," Clint offered.

"Nope. He's a cowboy and he said it was gonna be this mornin' and that is that. Besides, he'll probably be just as hung over tomorrow mornin' as this mornin'."

Clint shook his head. "Seems a shame that he gets drunk every night."

"Is a damn shame. But that don't mean he ain't a hell of a broncbuster anyway."

The morning started the same as most and it dragged on with the cowboys working their new horses, bucking them out a little, doing a little reining and generally waiting for Jepson. Clint could feel the excitement and it did not surprise him. The palomino stallion was a big, rangy horse with a lot of fire and spirit. It had a Roman nose and a narrow chest but moved with a restless and surging intensity that gave evidence of his being a real bucker. Actually, two cowboys had already tried the horse when Jepson and Ace were out of sight and both of them had gotten piled within three jumps and damned near stomped to death. The horse was an outlaw, a real killer.

It was about mid-morning when Jepson stumbled outside and stood on the veranda.

"There he is!" a cowboy named Billy said. "Let's get his saddle and gear out and cinch 'em down. From the looks of him, he can't afford to waste any strength."

Clint had to agree. Jepson looked like walking death. He was pasty-colored, like biscuit mix, and he stood on the veranda holding his head in pain. Milly came out and they began to argue. Then Jepson pushed her away and crammed his hat down low on his head. Clint heard the young man say, "I said I was going to ride that golden bastard, and I will, Milly."

"But why today!" Milly came hurrying over to Rafe. "Make him let someone else ride that killer!"

Rafe Longely shook his head. He feigned a sympathetic look. "You know I can't order your brother to do anything. I'm just the foreman, he's the boss's son, Milly. If Jepson wants to try the big stud horse, I can't stop him."

"You mean you don't want to stop him!" She whirled on Clint. "Please. Look at Jepson! He's not even in shape to ride a livery nag!"

"I'll have a talk with him," Clint said, knowing it wouldn't help. Jepson was a stubborn and pride-soaked fool. Now, with all the attention this was causing, he was the very center of things, which is exactly where he wanted to be.

Clint walked over to Jepson while they were saddling the stallion. He could hear the big animal tearing the hell out of the place.

"Listen," Clint said. "It ain't necessary to do this. Especially not today."

"You're not my brother-in-law yet, so mind your own damn business, Gunsmith."

"That's a dangerous horse. Some of the cowboys are saying he's an outlaw that will never be tamed. Why don't you turn him loose?"

Jepson knelt on one knee and tightened his stirrup straps. "Not a chance," he said through gritted teeth.

"Just for curiosity's sake, how is the betting?"

"About fifty-fifty," Clint said. "Most of the hands think you could do it if you were . . . were in shape."

"I'm sober."

"Sometimes that isn't enough."

"This ain't no gunfight I'm stepping into," Jepson reminded him. "It's just another horse."

"A killer. When you face a killer, Jepson, you have to be at your best. The stakes are your life."

Jepson straightened. His mouth twisted contemptuously. "You're just like my Pa," he said, glancing back toward the ranch house. "Always underestimating me. You watch close, Gunsmith. I'll show you how it's supposed to be done. Who knows, maybe there's even a trick or two in return you can teach me about gunfighting." He said it with the faintest hint of a smile and Clint nodded.

"Who knows? Good luck."

"Luck ain't got a damn thing to do with it," Jepson said as he moved toward the circular breaking corral.

Clint and Milly moved quickly to the corral as did all the other cowboys. Inside, the palomino stallion was tied to the snubbing post and it was fighting like hell. A cowboy jumped in and grabbed its ear and twisted hard while another covered the horse's eyes with a blindfold.

Jepson wasted no time getting on board. One minute he was sauntering across the dusty corral watching the proceedings, the next minute he was vaulting into his saddle and yelling for the cowboys to pull the blindfold and, "turn 'er loose!"

They did this gladly and sprinted for the safety of the corral fence. For a split second, the palomino seemed to freeze with indecision, then it squealed, ducked its head as far as Jepson would allow and sunfished into the sky.

Jepson hung on even though it seemed for an instant as if the palomino turned upside down. The next few minutes were the most brutal fighting between a man and a horse that Clint had ever seen. The palomino fought like a crazed thing. It swapped ends so fast that Jepson's head snapped like a limp whip. It pile-drived so hard that blood began to pour from Jepson's nose and foul his mustache. It reared up and went over backward but Jepson anticipated the move and jumped free at the very last instant. It did everything but reach up and pull the young broncbuster off of its back with its big corn-colored teeth.

But just when it seemed the outlaw stallion was ready to quit, it tried once more and, when it bucked, Jepson and his saddle broke from the startled horse and were thrown to the dirt.

"No!" Milly screamed as the palomino leapt at Jepson and came down on his chest. "No!"

Clint saw Jepson's body go into a spasm and blood run out of the corner of his mouth. Several cowboys tried to get inside but Clint knew they would never stop the outlaw stallion from killing Jepson. The horse was vicious and the worst killer Clint had ever seen. That's why he did the only thing that he could do and that was to pull out his six-gun and kill the crazed animal before it could stomp Jepson to pieces.

His gun came up and it sent two bullets into the horse's fevered brain. The palomino dropped, dead before it hit the dust.

Old Ace Hathaway came out of nowhere and was the first man into the corral. He picked up his son as if he were a broken rag doll and yelled, "Get a buckboard and let's get him to Dr. Cready! Hurry, you starin' sons-ofbitches!"

Clint didn't know how they got a team hitched so fast but it came slewing around the ranchyard only a few minutes later. They loaded Jepson into it and raced for Evansville with Ace using the whip and Milly and Rafe in the back of the buckboard holding Jepson down.

Everyone just stood in stunned silence and watched as the tail of dust receded into the horizon. "I don't think he has a prayer of reaching town alive," one cowboy said. Most of the men nodded.

"What do you think, Gunsmith? You seen a lot of shot and dead men. He got a chance?"

Clint shook his head. "I don't know," he said. "He looked real bad."

Someone brought Jepson's saddle over and swore, "Of all the sonofabitchin' bad luck. Look at that, a busted cinch!"

Clint absently glanced at the cinch and then he stared at it hard. He wasn't sure, but it almost looked as if . . . as if the cinch had been cut or purposely frayed with a knife's edge! He looked toward town. Maybe, he thought, keeping his suspicions to himself, bad luck had nothing at all to do with it.

TWENTY

Clint sure didn't feel like riding out his rough stock and he guessed no one else in the outfit did either. But those broncs he had been given were his responsibility so he saddled the big old roan with feet the size of dinner plates and a head like a keg of nails. He'd ridden it twice already and, though the animal was too muscle-bound and clumsy to be a great bucker, it was stout enough to jerk a man's arm half out of its shoulder socket.

When he stepped into the saddle, the roan grunted and tried to ram its head down. It halfway succeeded and then set off to crow hopping around and around the corral in bucks that a kid could have handled but which were surprisingly stiff and jarring. It was on the sixth or seventh jump that Clint's right stirrup broke and he went flying. One minute he was riding high, wide and handsome, the next he was smashing into the pole corral and seeing stars.

He woke up in the bunkhouse with a throbbing pain in his left forearm, the kind that told him he'd suffered a cracked or broken bone.

"You'll live," Smitty said, "but you got a couple of knots on your head the size of horse-turds. And that arm of yours is all swelled up and gettin' purple. But it ain't your gun arm and, like I said, you'll live."

Clint pushed himself up and groaned. "What happened?"

A cowboy toted Clint's saddle into the bunkhouse and set it down at his feet. Without a word, he turned it over to show where the stirrup leather had been cut.

Clint's face grew hard and unrelenting. "Rafe did this," he growled. "And unless I miss my bet, he also scraped a knife blade back and forth across Jepson's cinch until its fibers parted."

"You got no proof of that," Billy said. He was one of the few men who seemed to genuinely admire rather than fear Rafe.

Clint cradled his aching head in his hands. "You're absolutely right, Billy. I haven't any proof and it doesn't seem too likely that I'll get any. But sometimes a man has to do what he knows is right. I can't let Rafe keep doing this kind of thing. He may have already caused Jepson to die. And I figure to be next."

Clint could tell by the faces of the cowboys that his words rang true. He'd won them over from Rafe and though he still guessed he'd never be a real cowboy himself, he would never again feel like he'd embarrass himself around them on a roundup or a trail drive. He'd learned a lot but now it was about time that he started to demonstrate what he knew best—bringing a man like Rafe Longely up short before he did any more damage.

"So what are you goin' to do about him, Gunsmith?" Smitty asked.

"I guess I'm going to see Jepson first. I just hope that Doc Cready can save him. After that, I'm going to face up to Rafe and let him decide what he wants to do."

"With a broken arm!" Billy exclaimed.

Clint struggled and managed a smile. "Like you said, it isn't my gun arm."

They nodded and Smitty said, "Rafe is damn good with a gun but I guess you must be better. Thing of it is, he probably figures it that way too. And Rafe ain't the kind of a man who does somethin' to lose."

"Does he use a knife or a hide-out gun?"

"Both. And he's good with a whip and a lariat."

"And a rock," Billy added, looking a little sheepish when someone gave him a strange look for mentioning such a thing. "Rafe has the best damn arm I ever saw on a man. He can throw a horseshoe a country mile. Hit a damn bird on the wing."

"Thanks," Clint said. "But there has never been a rock thrower yet that could match the speed of a .45 slug from my Colt."

They helped him into town and he went straight to the doctor's office where Ace, Milly and Rafe were waiting. Ace looked a hundred years old and Rafe looked up at Clint with surprise and unconcealed hatred.

"My God!" Milly cried when she saw Clint's battered face and left arm hanging limply in a sling. "What happened?"

Clint glared at Rafe. The man tensed expectantly but Clint turned away, ignoring him. What he had learned during his years as a sheriff was that the smart man chose his time and his place to fight. The very last thing Clint wanted right now was to have a blazing gun battle in Dr. Cready's outer office while the man was working feverishly to save young Jepson's life.

"I had a little accident. But never mind that, how is Jepson?"

Milly shook her head. "He's still inside with the doctor. It's bad, Clint."

Ace got up from his chair and came over to Clint.

"We don't know if he'll make it or not," he whispered
in a hoarse voice. "But he'd be dead for sure if you
hadn't shot that stud horse in a hell of a hurry. I owe
you, Gunsmith."

"No you don't."

"Yes I do. And I'll tell you this. Milly is in love with
you and I told her she can marry you once this is all
over. I'll be proud to have you for a son."

Clint didn't quite know what to say when Milly put
her arms around his neck and began to cry. It was obvious that Ace just naturally assumed any man with half
a brain would leap at the chance to marry his pretty girl.
And the old cattleman was almost right. But Clint still
wasn't ready to get married. Yet, he was plenty wise
enough to understand that this was not the time to make
excuses.

"Thanks," was all Clint said.

Rafe was on his feet, big fists balled and he was ready
to fight. "If that sonofabitch marries your daughter,
Ace, I'm packin' my freight back to Texas, goddamn
you!"

Ace whirled around and caught his foreman by surprise with a punch so hard that Rafe crashed through
the front window and into the street. Clint shoved Milly
away and went for his gun, fully expecting a hail of
bullets to come flying into the office.

But he was wrong. Rafe, his face and hands cut by the
shattered glass, was racing down the street toward his
horse.

"Maybe I better go back to the ranch," Clint said.
"He's liable to raise hell."

"No," Ace said. "As soon as I learn something about
my son, I'll go. It's my ranch and he's got some back
pay comin' to him and a whole lot more. I owe that man

plenty for all the years of bustin' his butt. I'll pay him off in money, horses or cattle enough to start his own spread down in Texas where he belongs."

The door to the examination room opened and Dr. Cready stepped outside. His gown was covered with blood. He looked at Ace and said, "Mr. Hathaway, the good news is that I think Jepson's lungs haven't been punctured by his fractured ribs. And if there isn't any internal bleeding, I think Jepson has a better than fifty–fifty chance of surviving."

Ace almost broke down. His knees buckled a little and he had to be helped to a chair. He didn't make any sound, but one could see how deeply he cared for the son he had never shown much affection toward.

"Is my boy awake?" Ace said.

Dr. Cready replied, "He's drifting in and out of consciousness. Ace, I haven't told you the bad news yet."

The old cattleman's head shot up and he climbed to his feet. Jaw corded with muscle, he waited stoically.

Dr. Cready cleared his throat. He was not a man who minced words and he came right to the point. "The bad news is that his pelvis is broken in three or four places. In fact, I believe you might say it's crushed."

Ace just blinked with incomprehension. Then he yelled, "What the hell is the damned pelvis?"

The doctor took a backward step. "I'm sorry, that's his hip. He's lucky the horse came down with its weight there instead of his abdom . . . his belly, or his spine. In the first case he'd have ruptured inside, in the second case he'd be paralyzed."

"What about this here . . . pelvic?" Ace demanded.

"Pelvis. It should heal in time. But he'll never run or ride a horse again without some pain. In the winter cold, it will probably ache."

Ace slammed his big fist into the palm of his hand. "Never ride a horse without pain? Hell, that boy is the greatest horseman I ever saw and I mean he can outride any man alive!"

"Why don't you go tell him that before you go back to the ranch, Pa?" Milly whispered.

The fury drained right out of Ace and he looked a little nervous. But when the doctor said, "It would help, Mr. Hathaway. The young man has a destructive tendency and, without your support, he may not try hard enough to live."

"Then I'll do it," Ace said, pushing his way into the examining room and moving to Jepson's side. He took his son's hand in his own and bent close over Jepson and whispered for a long while.

Milly was weeping silently and, when Jepson raised his hand and softly patted his father's shoulder, Clint got such an ache in his throat he couldn't swallow.

A moment later, Ace Hathaway was striding past them and he looked as if he had dropped twenty years off himself. There was a spring in his step and a jut to his jaw.

"You can't imagine what that did for Pa," Milly said. "I've always known I was his favorite, but that he still loved Jepson very, very much. He just couldn't tell him until now."

Clint nodded and followed her in to the examination room. Jepson looked like death, but when he winked, he proved he wanted to live again.

A young girl rushed into the outer office. "Jep!" she cried. "Jep!"

Her face was smeared with tears and makeup and she was obviously not a preacher's daughter. But she was just as obviously distraught over the news of Jepson's accident.

"Who are you?" the doctor demanded.

Milly stepped between them. "It's about time we met. You're the girl named Cherry that my fool brother talks about in his sleep."

Cherry burst into a fresh torrent of tears.

The doctor glowered at the two women and then turned his attention to Clint. "Let's have a look at that busted arm, Gunsmith. As if I haven't enough to worry about. Five more men like you and I'd be rich."

Clint just shrugged and said, "I hope this is the last time I have to pay you a visit. But I won't bet on it."

The doctor removed the sling and gently rolled up the sleeve of Clint's shirt. He whistled softly. "Gunsmith," he said after he examined it, "the good news is I don't need to amputate the damned thing but the bad news is that it's broke in two places."

Clint nodded. "Just put a splint on it and bandage her up. I got things to attend to."

"Not today, you don't. That head and this arm say you need at least one good night's rest. And that's doctor's orders!"

"Okay," Clint said. "I reckon Milly and me will want to stay here close to Jepson anyway."

"Can I stay too?" Cherry asked with a sniffle. "I love him too much to leave. If it's improper, I'll just wait outside and . . ."

Milly shook her head and whispered, "You'll wait right here with us."

TWENTY-ONE

It was after dark when Rafe rode slowly into the ranchyard. Normally a prideful man, he looked as if he'd fought a dozen Comanche single-handed. His face and hands were cut up and the side of his face where Ace Hathaway's massive fist had exploded was puffy and misshapen.

To bury his anger and his killing hatred for the way he'd been pushed aside for a man no better than the Gunsmith, Rafe had spent the entire afternoon and evening drinking and visiting the whores. He probably spent three month's wages, but it hadn't made him feel a damn bit better. The wounds cut too deep.

Why, there had even been a time when he and Ace had been like father and son. They'd been closer by far than had Ace and Jepson. But it all just went to prove that blood was thicker than water, and when it came right down to the tough choices, a man would desert another man unless he was kinfolk.

Rafe dismounted and moved into the barn. He unsaddled his lathered horse and started to put his gear away but then he stopped and had an idea. He'd been ramrodding this spread for almost five years, working six and seven days a week for not much more than an ordinary cowboy's wages. He'd been willing to do it because he'd always figured that Milly Hathaway would be his bride. Later on, he could figure out some way to run off Jepson and take over the entire ranch. But now that he was left out in the cold, Rafe believed that he was owed and owed plenty. It was time to collect.

He went out into the corral behind the barn and selected the two fastest horses on the ranch. Then, he took them inside the barn, saddled both and grained them heavy. Blood was thicker than water and with the kind of money, silver and jewelry Rafe knew he'd find inside the ranch house, he could return to his home range down in Texas and start his own spread. He'd be the wealthiest Longely in the hill country of Texas—unless some of his kinfolk had taken up robbing banks instead of just rustling horses and cattle.

The lights in the bunkhouse were extinguished and when the horses had eaten their oats, Rafe put big canvas saddlebags on them and led both animals around to the back of the house and tied them to the water pump. There weren't even any locks on the doors. Ace had probably figured any man bold enough to get past his men and enter the ranch house would deserve whatever loot he could get away with.

Rafe entered by the kitchen door and struck a match though he probably could have walked through the house blindfolded without knocking anything over. He really had been one of the family not so long ago. And if the goddamn Gunsmith hadn't come along, he still would be. I should have killed the man myself the first day I saw him with Milly, he thought with bitterness. Instead, I tried to let Jerome do the job, then a damn bronc. I should have taken care of him way back then.

Rafe moved through the huge living room and down the hall past the bedrooms until he came to the study where Ace kept his operating cash and valuables. There was no safe so Rafe knew the man would put them in his rolltop desk. Ace wasn't very crafty; it would never even occur to him that anyone would try to steal his money.

The cash was in a thick brown paper envelope and Rafe felt his pulse quicken as he counted out five thousand dollars and change. He shoved the money into his coat pocket. When longhorn cattle in Texas were bringing in less than six dollars a head, five thousand dollars went a long, long way toward building a big herd, hiring some cowboys and buying a ranch.

The hand-carved jewelry box Rafe found was made of polished cherry wood with brass fittings and a small keyhole. Strangely enough, it was locked. Rafe searched for a little brass key and when he found none, he ground the box to pieces under his boot heel and out tumbled a beautiful diamond wedding ring, a diamond necklace, a jade pendant and diamond earrings.

Rafe stared at them knowing they were probably worth more than the cash. He remembered seeing Mrs. Hathaway wearing them in her coffin and it had never occurred to him that they might have been removed before the burial. But they were probably heirlooms and would have been Milly's upon her wedding. "Maybe she'll just have them anyway," he said, shoving them into his other coat pocket. He cleared away the splinters of wood and deposited them in a wastepaper basket.

Rafe studied the room. It was man-sized and he remembered how many good times he and Ace had sitting here on the leather furniture, smoking expensive Cuban cigars and drinking St. Cruiz rum from the crystal decanter. Rafe had loved those times. The two men had always talked of cattle and horses, of plans concerning the ranch. Jepson had never been there, but often Milly had

been. It had been so damned easy to get hooked into be-
lieving it would all belong to him and Milly some day.

A bitter twist cut Rafe's thin lips and he moved over
to the humidor on Ace's desk and pulled out all the
man's cigars. Then, he walked over and took the crystal
decanter of rum and drank it straight. The rum was as
smooth as molasses and it fired his blood and glowed
hotly in his belly.

He was sloshing the rum across his cut hands and
patting it on his lacerated cheeks when he heard the
drumbeat of a horse's hooves enter the ranchyard. Rafe
hurried to the window and he gently pushed the curtains
aside to see the unmistakable form of Ace dismounting
and leading his horse into the barn.

Rafe stepped back in momentary panic. What the hell
was Ace doing here with his son lying near death! Rafe
had a wild impulse to return everything to the drawers
and run out the back door. Tomorrow morning, he
could get up, collect his back pay from Ace and ride on
out.

But then, he remembered the shattered jewelry box
and the cigars in his pockets and the rum spilled so care-
lessly all over the floor. Rafe took a deep breath and
knew there was no turning back now.

He had to kill Ace and ride for Texas.

Ace came inside and lit a lantern, then moved toward
his bedroom. He walked slowly, like a tired old man.
His mind was distracted, thinking about his son and the
years wasted between them. The boy would live. They
would become like father and son again. Like they were
when Jepson was entering his teens.

I'll make it up to him, Ace thought. He's my blood
and, along with Milly, the future of everything I've
worked for my whole life. The Gunsmith will set a bet-

ter example than I have for the boy. Everything is going to be better now. Maybe this whole accident thing was a blessing in disguise.

Ace stepped through the door into his bedroom feeling the years weighing down on his powerful shoulders. Funny, but he would be seventy years old next month. Never thought he'd live to be seventy, considering the hell-raising he'd done, the Indians he'd fought, the outlaw horses he'd busted. But he'd never been the horseman that Jepson was right now, never in his best days.

Ace noticed that there was a candle flickering on his washstand beside his wife's picture. Now why . . .

Rafe brought the barrel of the heavy Winchester rifle down on the top of the cattle baron's head with all his strength. The impact of steel and bone was so great that his powerful arms shook. When Ace crashed to the floor, Rafe knew that no man, not even this one, could survive such a crushing blow.

He dropped the rifle and stared down at Ace. He willed himself to turn the man over with the toe of his boot. For a moment, Rafe was almost overcome with remorse. He almost whispered, "Pa."

Instead, he knelt and rifled through the old man's pockets until he found his wallet and emptied it. Rafe stripped Ace of a big gold ring that he had admired for years and just knew would fit his own hand. He was wrong, though, the ring was too big. Rafe shoved it into his pants pocket figuring he could get it cut down to size later.

Rising to his feet, Rafe grabbed the old man by the ankles and dragged him down the hallway and back into the study. He splashed the remainder of the rum across the body and the rugs, then lit a match and dropped it and headed for the back door.

Within minutes, he was galloping toward Evansville pulling the extra saddlehorse. No one would catch him, no one would even be able to prove he'd come and gone.

When he was a mile out into the darkness, Rafe reined his horse to a stop and watched the flames as they clawed like burning fingers up through the windows toward the rooftop. He could see small, dim figures racing about in the yard and he knew they would be forming a bucket brigade in a valiant but hopeless attempt to put out the fire.

"If I can't live in the sonofabitch," Rafe whispered, "and make love to Milly in one of them beds, nobody else will either."

He had the money, the jewelry and the ring. Now, all he wanted was the girl. She'd come to love him down in Texas and, by damned, she'd better, or there were both men and women kinfolk aplenty down in Texas to tan her hide and show her the way to behave.

Rafe pulled out one of the fine Cuban cigars from his coat pocket. He bit off the tip and licked it up and down before shoving it between his teeth and lighting it. His face glowed with the match light and he was smiling.

TWENTY-TWO

Milly kissed the Gunsmith good night and pulled the nightcovers over him.

"I still say I ought to wait down in the doctor's office with you just in case."

"In case what?" she asked. "Jep is going to be all right. And you've a broken arm and lumps all over your head. You need sleep, Clint. If there were anything you could do to help, then I'd say so—but there isn't. Besides, what have you to talk about with Cherry and me?"

"Not much." He frowned but resigned himself to her logic. Besides, his head and busted arm both ached like a couple of stubbed toes and he desperately wanted to sleep.

"Wake me up for breakfast," he said with a yawn.

"I will."

"Clint? Everything is going to be good for us. I really do love you."

He kissed her tenderly. "We need to talk some, Milly. I'm still not ready to . . ."

She seemed to guess what he was going to say and she placed her forefinger over his lips. "Don't say anymore, Clint. Not tonight."

"Okay."

He watched her leave the room and, in truth, he was beginning to think that maybe he would marry this girl someday. Not tomorrow or the next, but somewhere down the line. Getting married was a big jump for a confirmed bachelor. The idea just took a lot of getting used to.

Milly walked down the stairs of the hotel where Clint was staying the night, and out into the fresh night air. She took a deep breath and started toward the doctor's office. Her first concern was Jepson and her second concern was whether or not Clint Adams would marry her. She was certain that he would but she knew that such a man could not be crowded or he might bolt and run. I have to give him time, she thought. If he feels too much pressure, he'll resist.

That settled in her mind, Milly turned her thoughts to Cherry. She had previously seen the girl in town, but only at a distance. Cherry was really quite nice-looking. It was obvious she did have a certain charm that Milly could believe men found attractive. The idea of her being a prostitute was going to take some getting used to and she would have to serve as a buffer between Ace and the girl.

But it was clear that Cherry loved her brother and he badly needed to be loved, to have some kind of stabilizing influence in his wasted life. Cherry could be that influence and she was smart. In the short time they'd talked, Milly learned that the girl could read and write and had gone to school almost to the eighth grade. So, she was pretty well educated and if . . .

"Rafe!" Milly said, startled by the appearance of the big man who stepped out of the shadows into her path. "What are you doing here?"

"I wanted to talk to you alone for a few minutes, Milly. I wanted to tell you something important before I go away."

Because of the terrible cuts on his face and hands and the almost pleading in his eyes, Milly found herself nodding. Once, she'd actually considered marrying this man. He loved her deeply, she was certain of that though she suspected he also greatly coveted marrying into the ranch and its wealth.

"Can we just step off the boardwalk and go for a little walk?"

She did not want to go for a walk with this man. "I can't go far," she said as he took her hand. "Jepson is very bad and I might be needed."

"I know that," he said. "It's a hell of a thing that happened. He should never have tried to ride the horse in his condition. He drinks too damn much, Milly."

"I know that. But that is not of concern right now. What did you want to talk to me about?"

They were walking toward the Lion River. "I wanted to see if you'd elope with me," Rafe said.

"Are you crazy!"

He stopped and his hand tightened on hers until it hurt. "No, goddammit! Can't you understand that I'm in love with you? Don't that mean anything?"

Milly felt an icy chill sweep through her body. She realized that she would have to be very careful. "I'm sorry. Yes, I know you love me, but . . . well, I don't love you, Rafe. I'm in love with the Gunsmith."

He rocked back as if she'd slapped him and Milly could see the way he struggled to stay under control.

"He ain't worthy of you! All he wants is a pasture to retire in. He can't run the ranch. Not like I can! Milly, I'm begging you to reconsider."

"I'm very sorry," she told him sincerely. "But I don't love you."

"You might, in time. You see, down in Texas . . ."

"No!" she said, trying to pull her hand from his. "Why can't you just accept the fact that I'm in love with the Gunsmith. Rafe . . ."

"What?" he demanded. "What were you going to say to me just now?"

Milly took a deep breath. She had to make this man understand how deeply she loved the Gunsmith. She had to sever whatever infatuation he had for her. "I was going to say that I have been making love to the Gunsmith. I'm his woman, Rafe. He knows me inside and out."

It was clear that he had not allowed himself to believe it. Now, his face contorted in rage and he drew back his fist and hissed. "That's a lie, Milly!"

"No!" she cried, fighting to pull away from him. "He's had me at least . . ."

The fist traveled only six inches but when it struck her eye, Milly dropped and spun into a dark hole. Rafe caught her and carried her to his horse. He threw her roughly across the extra saddlemount, tied her down and said, "Since you already acted like a common whore, I'll treat you like one, Miss Milly Hathaway. And I'll be doing you the favor of your life to marry you. There will come a day when you will beg me for forgiveness. I swear there will be!"

Rafe jammed his boot into his own stirrup and swung into the saddle. Unmindful of the beating that Milly would take, he spurred his horse hard and sent it and Milly's horse into a gallop. Texas was his home and, by damn, Milly was going to be his woman.

TWENTY-THREE

When the Gunsmith awoke the following morning, he felt surprisingly refreshed. His arm still throbbed but he had suffered enough broken limbs to realize that the throbbing would gradually diminish and finally disappear altogether within the next few days. When he shaved before the mirror, he noticed that the knots and bruises on his face and head were also disappearing. "You won't win any beauty prizes for a few more weeks, but at least you won't cause dogs to howl when they see you coming," he told himself.

Clint dressed and buckled on his gun. It was almost eight o'clock and he was surprised that Milly had not awakened him already. He was famished but he hurried over to the doctor's office and ignored his rumbling belly.

"Clint," Cherry said, arising from her chair looking worn and wearing dark circles under her eyes. "You look much better than you did last night."

He wished he could say the same for Cherry. "How's Jepson?" he asked, moving into the examining room where Jepson lay sleeping. "He looks better. He's not so pale anymore."

"Dr. Cready was in about midnight but then he got a call and rushed out. Something about trouble at the

Hathaway Ranch. That's where I thought maybe you and Milly went.''

Clint blinked with surprise. "Wasn't she here all night?"

"Why no. I thought she and you . . ." Cherry swallowed. "Maybe she went to the ranch with her father."

Clint shook his head violently as he spun for the doorway. "She wouldn't leave Jepson while he was this badly hurt.''

Clint raced over to the livery where Duke was being kept. Because of his broken arm, he had the liveryman saddle his black gelding and he rode Duke hard all the way to the Hathaway Ranch.

He smelled the smoke miles before he even reached the ranch headquarters. It filled him with dread and when he came within sight of the ranch, his worst fears were realized.

"What happened?" he shouted as he galloped into the ranchyard.

They were a sad looking bunch. Bleak and vacant-eyed and filled with genuine grief. Slowly, like men in shock, they told Clint the story. "There were two horses that came in after dark. Some of us heard them. It had to be Ace and Miss Hathaway. And then, not more than fifteen minutes after the second horse came, there was the fire. By the time we smelled smoke and got outside, the whole ranch house was ablaze. Flames shooting up through the rooftop, embers flying everywhere. Wasn't nothing we could do to stop it. Both the boss and poor Miss Hathaway burned to death, Gunsmith.''

Clint walked over to the huge rectangle of ashes. It was still smoldering but he ignored the heat and smoke and trudged through the rubble. It didn't take long to find the human skeleton and, from its unusual size, it was pretty obvious it was either Rafe Longely or Ace Hathaway. Clint's lean face was grim. As a lawman, he'd seen this sort of thing at least a half-dozen times during his career but it never got any easier to stomach.

He began to look for the remains of Milly Hathaway. He picked up a hot rifle-barrel with the stock burned off and used it to poke and prod through the ashes.

"What you lookin' for?"

"Milly," he said tightly.

There were no more questions for the nearly two hours that he went over every square inch of the place until he was satisfied that Milly had not died there. Only then did he allow himself to relax a little bit. He had no proof at all, but how much did a man need? If Ace were alive, the man would have been visible either here or in town near his injured boy. So Ace had to be dead and the only one who'd do a thing like this was Rafe.

"You seen Rafe?" he asked the cowboys almost casually.

"No sir. He hasn't been here since you all took Jepson to town in the wagon after he'd been stomped near to death. How is he, Gunsmith?"

"Jepson is going to be alright," Clint said. "But there's a body in those ashes. It belongs to Ace Hathaway. Where does Rafe Longely hail from?"

"Texas."

"I know that!" Clint lowered his voice and realized how close to the breaking point he was. "What part of Texas?"

Billy spoke up. "You think Rafe had something to do with this?"

Clint had trouble keeping himself from shouting.

"What part of Texas?" he repeated in a flat voice.

"The hill country," Billy said. "Rafe told me the

Longelys are famous in those parts."

"I heard different," Smitty offered quietly.

"What do you mean by that?"

"Well, I heard that the Longelys are the most hated and dangerous family in those parts. Everyone is afraid of them. They run a town down there someplace. Own it outright and use it to harbor outlaws that come through."

Clint started for his horse. "I don't suppose you remember the name of that town."

"Longely," Smitty said. "Longely, Texas. And I hear there are about fifty of them and they are the meanest men in the state."

Clint shoved a boot into the saddle. It was awkward trying to mount a horse with one hand but he managed. "So long, boys," he said as he rode out.

They stared after him. Finally, Smitty paid him one of the greatest compliments of his life when the man yelled, "So long, cowboy!"

Clint put the spurs to Duke and headed back to Evansville. He would comb the town for Milly and if no one had seen or heard of her, he'd have to assume the very worst—that Rafe had taken the young cowgirl with him to Texas.

God help Milly survive whatever Rafe was going to do with her. And then, God help him and any other Longelys who got in the Gunsmith's path.

When Clint reached Evansville, he rode straight up to the doctor's office. Cherry's face wore a radiant expression until she saw the Gunsmith. His boots and pants were covered with ash and he looked grim and gaunt.

"Clint, what's wrong?"

"How is Jepson?"

"He's much better and wide awake. Clint, he asked me to marry him."

Jepson opened his eyes and waved them over to his side. "She said she'll have to think about it. Can you believe that? She doesn't think maybe I ought to marry someone who's been . . . well, you know."

"She's wrong," Clint said. "Some of the best women in the West had to earn their livelihoods in saloons. The smart ones that never gave up hope got married and had children. They made devoted wives. You ought to marry him, Cherry. Don't let foolish pride rob you of your chance for happiness. He needs you more than you need him."

"Thanks," Jepson said drily, "for telling her the truth. But the Doc says I'll never be able to break horses again."

"Hire men to do it. You're going to have to run the ranch now. All by yourself."

Jepson blinked. "Ace and Rafe are . . ."

"Gone," Clint interrupted. "Jepson, your father is dead. I'm almost certain that Rafe robbed and killed him."

Jepson covered his face with his hands for a moment. He took a long, shuddering breath and then swore, "I'll find Rafe and kill him if it takes me a hundred years!"

"No," Clint said. "It's my kind of work. You're a cowboy. A rancher's son. You've got a spread to take care of for Milly and . . ."

"For Milly? What is that supposed to mean?"

Clint wished he didn't have to say it but there was no choice. "It means that Milly is gone. I think that Rafe took her with him to Texas."

Jepson closed his eyes and clenched his fists. "And here I am, helpless as a damn baby and . . . we got to save her from that animal! Tell the men, they'll go with you and hunt him down. They all loved Milly."

"Uh-uh," Clint grunted. "You see, that would be exactly the wrong thing to do. All it would cause is a war and since we'd be on the Longely's home range, we'd lose. Hell, it'd be a needless slaughter of good Hathaway cowboys. Cowboys that know how to ride and rope and herd cattle but don't know beans about gunfighting."

"Then get a United States Marshal!"

"Take too long," Clint said. "And the odds are I'd be sending him to an early grave. No, I have to do this myself."

"But how?" Cherry asked. "If it's that dangerous, what chance would anyone have, even you?"

"I don't know." Clint bent down and patted Jepson on the shoulder. "You rest easy and get well; you have big shoes to fill. And don't worry, if it can be done, I'll bring Milly back safe. But if you don't see us within a month, send the U.S. Army to Longely, Texas. Either that, or contact a Seth Billings, of the Texas Rangers, and tell him about where I went and that I was killed."

"We'll wait the month, but you'll return long before that," Jepson said confidently. "I intend for you to be the best man at our wedding."

"And Milly must be my bridesmaid," Cherry said, almost shyly. "If she wouldn't mind."

"Milly will take it as an honor," Clint assured the girl.

He bid them farewell and headed for Mrs. Evans' general store. He was going a long ways and he needed some supplies. And just in case he never got back, he wanted to tell Dade's widow good-bye.

TWENTY-FOUR

Clint rode into Amarillo, Texas, four days later. He was tired and thickly coated with trail dust. His mood was sour because he still had a long way to go to reach the hill country of Texas and he was deeply concerned about Milly.

He'd thrown away the sling for his broken arm and when he was in the saddle, he just rested his left hand on his hip, hooking his thumb through his belt loop. When he dismounted, he tucked the arm inside his shirt or coat and while that made it look like he was continually scratching his belly, Clint didn't care. It was more comfortable than the sling and he figured the arm would heal better if it weren't always hanging in the same position. He used a leather pouch crammed with moss and squeezed it over and over to keep the muscles of his hand and forearm from withering.

Duke was played out because he'd been pushed hard. It had been eighteen months since Clint had ridden through the Texas panhandle country and the memory of his last visit was still vivid. There had been a little disagreement over a pretty café owner in town. Her name was Juliet and it seemed that she was the object of a jealous man's unwanted affections. Clint hadn't known that and when he'd taken Juliet out on the range for a

126

buggy ride, the toughest man in Amarillo had followed them out and challenged Clint to a gunfight.

Clint remembered very well how he'd tried to talk reason into the fool, whose name he'd completely forgotten. But when the jealous stranger had drawn his gun, Clint had no choice but to shoot to kill. The man had been damned fast, one of the fastest Clint had ever seen. They'd fired at almost the same instant but the difference was Clint's experience. His bullet had been true to the mark while his opponent's had been fired an eyelash too quickly and had grazed Clint's thigh. He still wore the scar and he still remembered how Juliet had wept that afternoon on the prairie.

I wonder if she still owns the café? he asked himself. Juliet had been a strikingly handsome redhead, quite tall and well built. Her only drawback was that she was the clumsiest woman Clint had ever known. She was forever dropping things. But Juliet had such a sweet smile and good sense of humor that everyone just naturally forgave her shortcomings. Besides, she was a terrific cook and storyteller. And so damned attractive that when a man saw her drop something or stumble over her own feet, he just naturally yearned to take Juliet into his arms and protect her from inflicting any more harm on herself. Juliet was the only girl that Clint had ever known that had calluses on her knees from spending so much time picking up things she had dropped and broken.

He bedded Duke down and headed for Juliet's Café. When he walked inside, there she was, as big as life and down on the floor and using a rag to mop up spilled coffee and broken glass. It kind of seemed fitting that he would catch her cleaning up another mess. Clint could not imagine how many dishes, cups and saucers Juliet broke each week, but it had to be at least a dozen. It was a good thing she owned this place; no one could afford to hire help like her.

Clint took a stool and waited until she finished cleaning and came to her feet. He couldn't help but smile at her. She was as pretty as ever and he'd forgotten how her smile even included her green eyes.

"Hello, Juliet," he said, turning around on the stool as she stood up with the tray of broken glass and coffee-soaked rags. "Remember me?"

She stared at him for a second, then squealed and threw herself at him. Clint saw her coming. He tried to get his left hand out of his shirt and get off the stool. He was too slow. Juliet's soft body struck him and before she could wrap him up tight in her strong arms, he was toppling to the floor, caught between his stool and the next.

"Oh Clint Adams!" she cried, spilling the tray over him as she bent to help him up. "I've missed you so much!"

He'd banged his broken arm on the edge of the counter as he fell and it was throbbing again. He'd bruised his tailbone and his elbow and when people in the café began to laugh at his ridiculous predicament, he didn't care much for that either. Maybe it served him right for forgetting that he needed to keep the counter between them when she was serving food or coffee.

"Help me outa here," he said, a little rougher than he'd meant to sound.

Juliet pulled him to his feet as easily as she could. She was almost six feet tall and when she looked into his eyes, they met on a direct line. She put her arms around his neck and kissed him wetly. "You look too thin!" she scolded, pinching his sunken cheek. "And what's the matter with your arm?"

"Ouch! Don't touch it! It's broken—maybe all over again."

Juliet was not one to take offense at small criticisms. "Oh, Gunsmith! You always were getting yourself all banged up over one thing or the other."

He brushed the dirt from his clothes. "How about some food? Lots of steak and potatoes with gravy. And maybe some apple pie if you have any for desert."

Juliet had always loved to feed a man well. And whenever she saw one on the thin side, it seemed to evoke all her deepest sympathies.

"I'm gonna fatten you up so good," she vowed, "that by the time you leave here you'll waddle instead of walk."

"I can't stay," he said, regretting that he didn't have the time to let her do as she promised.

"Then you better eat continuously until you have to go."

Clint nodded. He was hungry enough to eat a horse and the food smelled damn good.

Clint had eaten too much but neither that nor his broken arm got in the way of things when it came time for making love with Juliet. She had big, lovely breasts and when she wrapped her long legs around his waist and began to buck and heave her body against his, Clint remembered another reason why Juliet was such a good woman to be around.

Clint took her from the top and later, from underneath as she squatted down and began to rise and fall onto him, impaling herself with delicious enjoyment.

"Oh, Clint," she breathed as she moved up and down with increasing speed, "why can't you at least stay a few more days with me? I'll fatten you up in the daytime and make you slick and happy in the nighttime."

He gazed up at her, admiring all that fine womanhood and pleased at how much she was obviously enjoying their lovemaking. "Why aren't you married yet?" he asked. "You're not only passionate and beautiful, but you're also a woman of some means. You must get a ton of offers every week."

"Uhhhh, that's nice," she groaned, her eyes almost closed. "Yes, I get offers, but not from you. Why haven't *you* gotten married?"

"I'm supposed to," he said.

Her movement stopped and she looked down at him with alarm and then started to climb off his stiff shaft. "I won't make love to another woman's husband or fiancé!"

He grabbed her by the hip and held her in place. "I'm not engaged," he said. "And I never promised I'd get married."

She relaxed and began to move on him again. "Oh . . . oh! That felt good!"

"Then don't stop."

She leaned forward so that he could take one of her breasts in his mouth and tongue her turgid nipple. And almost as soon as he did, she began to shudder and buck hard.

Clint grinned happily and forgot the throbbing ache of his left arm. It had always been easy to bring her to climax; her breasts were the key to her desire. Before she stopped bouncing up and down and yelling, Clint drove into her strongly until his body had emptied itself into her hot depths. She howled like a cat, and then purred like a milk-fed kitten.

"It's sure a good thing to see you again, Julie," he said as she toppled over on the bed beside him and landed on his broken arm.

"Ahhhh!" he bellowed.

She remembered at once but the damage was done. Clint ground his teeth as wave after wave of pain swept across the back of his eyes. Dammit! Juliet was beautiful, passionate and generous but she was dangerous to any man's health. Maybe that was why she had never married. Or maybe she had married and her poor husband had gotten himself killed because of her clumsiness. Either way, it sort of explained why she was still single.

"Clint?"

"Yes?"

"There's something you might want to know."

"What's that?"

"There's this man. The younger brother of the one you outdrew and shot the last time we were together."

"Yes."

"Well, he's vowed to kill you if you ever pass through this way again."

"All the more reason for me to get an early start."

Juliet rolled over and studied him in the candlelight. "I'm afraid it might already be too late."

He sat up fast. "What do you mean?"

"I mean, his best friend was eating at my place when you came in. I said your name and . . . well, he didn't even finish his apple pie. And you know how good my pie is."

Clint knew damn well how good it was because he'd

eaten three slices. "I better get to riding then," he said.
"I don't want to kill any more men than I'll already
have to down in Longely. You should have told me this
earlier, Juliet."

"I know," she confessed. "But I thought that if I
did, you'd rush off hungry and . . . well, unsatisfied. If
you know what I mean."

"Of course I do." He began to get dressed. "What
was the name of the man that I had to kill in self de-
fense?"

"Mose."

"What's the younger brother's name?"

"Ben Adler."

"I never heard of him," Clint said. "Is he supposed
to be fast on the draw?"

"Yes. Faster even than his late brother."

Clint swallowed. "I can't allow myself to get shot,"
he said, yanking on his boots. "I have to save Milly
Hathaway from Rafe Longely."

"Are you going to marry her?"

"No."

"Then will you come back here to visit me so I can
love you and fatten you up?"

He shook his head. "Not as long as there's an Adler
brother that is out to nail my hide to the headboard."

"I almost wish I hadn't told you," Juliet said with a
twinge of bitterness. "You outdrew Mose, I'm sure you
can outdraw Ben as well."

Clint finished getting dressed. "Good night and good-
bye, Juliet. Tell you what, next time I'm passing by, I'll
sneak into this bedroom and wait for you right here."

"You better ask around in case I got married. You
could be in for a real big surprise."

"Good point," he said, strapping on his gun and heading for the door.

Juliet sat crouched on her bed as naked as the day she was born. It took a strong-willed man to leave a woman like that, but there was not only his own life to consider losing, but the fate of Milly was resting entirely on his shoulders.

He left Juliet's cute little house and hurried toward the livery. Glancing up at the moon and stars, he guessed it was only about ten o'clock in the evening. He would ride for two hours and bed down on the prairie. It was a shame to miss out on all the loving and eating but Clint was a man who prided himself on thinking and acting responsibly.

And he was not one damn bit interested in facing the very fast gun of young Ben Adler.

TWENTY-FIVE

He had to wake the liveryman up and shake him out of his bed. "What the hell you want at this hour of the night!" the man raged.

"My saddle and bridle. I can't find them."

"That's because I lock them up at night so people like you can't sneak out in the night without paying their board bill."

Clint dug into his pocket and dropped a silver dollar on the man's chest. "Saddle and bridle my horse and do it fast."

The man bit the silver dollar, then smiled. "Yes sir!"

Clint was nursing his broken arm and wishing that Juliet hadn't fallen on top of it. He should have been paying more attention but . . .

"Put your damn hands up and turn around slow!"

Clint froze. He raised his right hand slowly.

"Both hands!"

"I can't. My left arm is broken," he grunted.

"How would you like to have it shot off!"

Clint managed to raise it above his shoulder.

"Now, turn around slow and easy."

"Ben, don't you kill him in my barn! Don't you do it, I say!"

"Shut up and go back to bed," Ben said, waving his

pistol in the man's general direction and sending him leaping into the nearest stall for cover. "So you're the man that killed my brother. The famous Gunsmith."

Clint faced a man of about his own size. Lean, good-looking, with wavy black hair and a square jaw. He didn't look to be much over twenty years old. "Some people call me that."

"But I call you a killer. And I don't believe that you gave my brother, Mose, a fair chance."

"Maybe you should ask Juliet."

"I did! But of course she lied. Mose was fast, faster than you ever thought about being."

Clint's left arm was really hurting him so he lowered it.

"Put it back up!"

"Go to hell," Clint hissed, easing his left hand into the front of his shirt. It felt better almost at once. "If you're going to shoot me down without giving me a fair chance, then I might as well die comfortably. If you're going to give me a chance, like your brother did, the left hand can't work against you anyway since its broken and my gun is on my right hip."

Ben Adler frowned. Then, he surprised Clint by shoving his gun back into his holster. He spread his feet apart a little and tensed. "All right, Gunsmith, you're going to have to prove to me that you were faster than Mose. There's only one way to do that, so draw your gun when you're ready."

"I can't do that," Clint said. "It would probably mean the death of Milly Hathaway. She's an innocent girl who's been kidnapped and I came to Texas to save her. If I lost, you'd be killing two people, not one."

It was obvious that Ben hadn't expected a complication like this. To him, drawing against the Gunsmith had been a simple act of seeking vengeance for his brother. Now, as he tottered at the brink of indecision, he shouted, "I don't believe you! You're making this up in order to save your own life!"

"No I'm not. It's the truth. The man who kidnapped her is named Rafe Longely. He's from Longely, Texas. I'd guess you have heard of that family."

"I heard more than I want to hear about them. They're outlaws and killers."

"I'm on my way to save the girl," Clint said. "I'll give you my word that I'll come back and face your gun if I can."

"I don't believe this!" Ben cried. "I've waited and practiced for over a year until the day I first heard of your whereabouts. And now, here you are and you won't draw on me."

He pulled out his gun and held it at arm's reach. He cocked it and aimed. "You're lying," he said.

Clint had to swallow, his throat was so dry. "If you kill me, you also kill a beautiful young woman. A woman now being held by the man who murdered her own father. A woman who will surely die trying to escape, for death would be preferable to bondage. Is that what you want?"

The gun began to waver in Ben's hand. "Dammit!" he shouted. "It wasn't supposed to go this way!"

"It never goes like it's supposed to," Clint said without sympathy. He turned his back on the young man and headed for Duke. "I'm leaving now. You can take my word I'll return or you can shoot me from behind."

"Dammit!" Ben bellowed in rage and frustration. "I'm coming with you!"

Clint set his feet into the stirrups and said, "If you come, you'll have to obey me to the letter. I won't allow some young hothead to get me and the girl killed. Is that clearly understood?''

Ben looked like he was going to explode. But he nodded his head and went for his horse.

And together, they struck out at a gallop for Longely, Texas.

TWENTY-SIX

Milly Hathaway thought of how she would rather die than spend the remainder of her life with Rafe. They had been riding hard for six days and she was mentally and physically exhausted. Rafe had been kind to her, more than kind, but she had ignored him.

He stopped his horse and pointed off toward some low, blue mountains that were still hazy in the distance. "See those hills?"

She nodded.

"That's the Texas hill country I've been telling you about," Rafe said proudly. "It's as pretty a country as you'll ever see. Better cattle country than your father had."

The word "had" jarred her like the gong of a brass bell. "What do you mean 'had'?" she demanded.

He realized the slip of tongue and said, "I was thinking about what I had, or almost had there at the Hathaway Ranch. You'd have married me if it hadn't been for the Gunsmith's coming to Evansville. Isn't that so?"

"I don't know," she said. "Between you and Pa, I never had a chance to get to know any other young men. I was afraid of becoming a spinster. All the young men were afraid of you and I blamed them for that. But Clint wasn't afraid."

"He'd never have made a good husband. You need a man who's more like your father was . . . I mean, is," Rafe amended quickly.

Milly looked at him sharply. "I think . . . I think you killed him," she said with a quavering voice.

"No!"

"You had to kill him to stop him from coming after us. Only death would have kept him away this long. Tell me the truth!" she screamed.

Rafe studied her a long time. "Alright," he said finally, "I did kill him."

The finality of those words was like a dull hammer striking Milly in the face. One minute she was staring at the Texan, hating him more than anyone she had ever known, and the next moment she was throwing herself off her horse and scratching at his eyes. Biting and clawing, cursing and wanting nothing more than to kill or be killed.

Rafe drew his gun and cocked it.

"Shoot me!" she cried. "Go ahead. I'll never love you. I'll see you dead first!"

Rafe almost believed her. If he had, he would have killed her right there on the prairie and been done with it. But he loved Milly and so he hesitated and then slammed the barrel of his pistol down on her head. She crumpled and he caught her before she dropped to the grass.

Rafe looked at the distant mountains. They were too far away to reach today anyway. He would make camp here and then take Milly home tomorrow. When his Pa and his brothers saw her, they'd understand why he would put up with such a fuss over a woman who hated him. But Ma, now she might be a little rough on Milly, Rafe thought. Ma was a mighty strong woman who didn't put up with much nonsense. Rafe knew that he might have to keep Milly away from his mother. She'd horsewhip Milly, peel the hide off of her if she did not behave.

Rafe dismounted and set about gathering buffalo chips for an evening fire. He kept glancing over at the girl, and just knowing that it was within his power to rape her whenever he wanted was the most exciting thought of his life. Before, when he thought of forcing Milly to make love, Ace had intruded on the vision. But not anymore. Ace was dead and burned to cinders. Milly was helpless and his to do with as he pleased.

Rafe was torn by his desire to run over and rape Milly, and yet on the other hand to protect her as Ace had once protected her. Milly hadn't really made love to the Gunsmith. She'd been lying, though for what reason Rafe could not imagine. Women were complicated creatures when you got to caring for them. The whores, well, who cared what they thought? But a girl like Milly, now that was another question entirely.

No sooner had Rafe built his campfire and got the coffee to boiling when three riders came galloping into view. They were moving fast toward New Mexico and when they saw Rafe, they reined toward his camp.

The big Texas cowman cussed. He wanted no visitors and three fast-moving strangers could mean big trouble. This was Comanche country and only hard men survived out here. This trio might be fleeing something and, if it were Indians, Rafe wanted to know about it now.

Rafe walked quickly over to Milly and covered her completely with a blanket. He checked his six-gun, his knife and the hide-out gun he kept hidden in the small of his back right behind his cartridge belt. It was a .32 caliber Smith and Wesson, a woman's gun really, but deadly at close range.

The men slowed their heavily lathered horses and one raised his hand in greeting. "Howdy!" he called, "we come in peace."

Rafe nodded. "Then ride on in."

They exchanged glances and said something that Rafe could not hear. They gigged their horses forward and Rafe studied them closely. They were all young and excited looking, wild and unkempt men with beards and dirty, sweaty faces. "That's far enough," he said when they were within twenty feet. "What can I do for you gents?"

"We need fresh horses."

"Can't help you. As you can see, we've only the two."

"Yeah, but two is better than none," the leader, a tall, thin young man who wore a red bandana said as he dismounted. He moved with the grace of a cougar and his pistol was low on his hip which might mean he was a professional gunfighter. "You see, we're in sorta a hurry."

"I can tell that by the looks of your mounts. Mind telling me why?"

"Yeah, I do," the man said.

Rafe stiffened. "If you're running from Comanche, me and my friend need to break camp and run too."

"Ain't runnin' from nothing, mister. We're just in a hurry is all. How much money will it take to make a swap?"

"I'm not interested. Out here, a man needs a good horse or he's in real trouble. If we get jumped by Indians, your money won't help me a damn bit."

One of the other men said, "Maybe we bein' too gentlemanly for you, mister. The thing of it is, we figure to take those two good-lookin' horses and if you don't offer us some food and whiskey, we might not leave our own in return."

Rafe took a deep breath. He carefully weighed the odds and how he was going to handle this situation. He had to assume these three were outlaws on the run and they knew how to draw and fire their guns in a handy sort of way. And while he figured he was probably faster than any of them, he had to also reckon that he could not outdraw and kill all three.

"Maybe I'm a little slow to catch onto things after all," Rafe said, forcing a disarming grin of friendship. "Hell, me and my friend got extra food and we ought to be able to come up with some kind of friendly swap."

"That sounds a whole lot better," the thin man with the fancy tied-down gun said, as he came forward. "We just are in sorta a fix and need fresh horses. Be better if we could swap all three but we have to do what we can until we find another."

"I understand," Rafe said, nodding vigorously. "And I'm sure we can work out a deal. You say you got cash?"

"Plenty enough," one of them said boastfully.

"Shut up, Dave," the thin leader said. "Just keep your damn mouth shut!"

"How about some coffee?" Rafe offered, noticing that the one named Dave wore a freshly blood-stained hole in his leather jacket.

"You bet. What's the matter with your friend?" he

asked, gesturing toward Milly's form outlined under the blanket. "He sick or something?"

"Yeah," Rafe said. "Real sick. Where you boys coming from?"

"Yonder," the thin one said, taking a tin cup and watching Rafe stir the boiling coffee. "You got any salt-pork or jerky we could eat? Been since yesterday that we had a meal."

"Sure," Rafe said, moving over to his saddlebags and being careful not to turn his back on the trio. This was all a deadly waiting game and he could feel his blood pounding. These boys might be gunslicks, but they had to be green or they'd have shot him as soon as they stepped off their exhausted horses. Shot him while they had the advantage of their numbers.

"Hey, that's a woman!" Dave yelled suddenly. "A damn good-looking woman, too!"

Rafe twisted around to see that Milly had regained enough consciousness to throw off the blanket he had covered her with. She was trying to get up but it was clear she was only dimly aware of the sudden excitement her presence caused among the three wolfish-looking strangers.

The third man moved toward her, his hands reaching just the way a kid's might when he saw a silver coin in the dust.

Now, Rafe thought, while they're all gawking at Milly!

Rafe's hand went down to the gun on his hip and his first bullet caught the reaching man just under the armpit. He went sprawling across Milly, who screamed. Dave and the thin gunfighter reacted with lightning speed. Both men drew and fired but Rafe's second bullet smashed into Dave and spilled him into the dirt.

The thin man really was a professional gunfighter and his first bullet caught Rafe in the arm and knocked him sideways. Rafe dropped to one knee in the swirling gun smoke and emptied his Colt. Dropping it, he reached behind his back, felt a bullet pluck at his shirt, rolled and drew the Smith and Wesson. Bullets were stitching the air all around him but Rafe fired the .32 caliber pistol until he saw the thin gunfighter crash over on his back and stop moving.

For several moments, nothing but the nervous horses made even the smallest sound. Then Milly grunted and pitched the dead man off her and climbed to her feet. She looked around at the carnage, turned her back on Rafe and walked out onto the prairie.

Rafe yanked the red bandana off the gunfighter and walked out to Milly. "Here," he said roughly, "you're my woman now, so bandage up my goddamn arm!"

Milly stared at him with hatred, but overriding fear made her obey.

A quarter of an hour later they started riding south again, moving as fast as they could with three riderless horses traveling behind. Rafe had found the saddlebags of the three men filled with cash and it was clear they were bank robbers. He had not taken the time to count the money but he figured it totaled at least two or three thousand dollars. My luck has changed for the good, he thought. I'll come home with more money than anyone in my family ever saw at one time. And with the best-looking hunk of woman in Texas.

Rafe ignored the pain in his wounded arm. The dying gunfighter's bullet had passed through the muscle cleanly and Ma would know how to fix a poultice and draw out any infection. She would teach Milly how to do that sort of thing.

Rafe glanced back over his shoulder at the three still bodies lying on the prairie. Had they been experienced men and shot first, he'd be lying out there instead of them. The fools would now have all the Hathaway money and the Hathaway girl. Sometimes, Rafe thought, youth and inexperience were life's most fatal handicaps.

TWENTY-SEVEN

"Well," Clint said, "there it is, Longely, Texas. There will be no turning back once we ride into their stronghold."

"I've no intention of turning back on anything," Ben said, his meaning crystal clear. Since leaving Amarillo, they had not spoken much to each other. Ben was determined to have his chance to kill the Gunsmith and Clint was too preoccupied with trying to figure out how he could rescue Milly to pay attention to the younger man.

Clint thought that having Ben at his side was a mixed blessing. It seemed, from the few questions that Ben asked, that he was genuinely honest and well-intentioned. He also seemed morally offended that Milly Hathaway could be abducted by force. Clint supposed the young gunfighter really would stand and fight the Longelys if necessary in order to recover Milly and preserve her honor. There was an undeniable streak of chivalry in Ben Adler.

But then again, Ben might be all talk. He just might break and run if the odds grew too unfavorable. Clint had seen a lot of men who acted that way—plenty of high-sounding talk until bullets started flying and the chances of surviving looked slim to none. That's why the Gunsmith knew he had to act as if he were all alone.

If it turned out that Ben was a man of courage and met the test, so much the better, but he could not afford to risk his own life or Milly's on that possibility.

"Anything more you want to tell me about the Longely's that might be useful?" Clint asked, as they rode on down to the small frontier town nestled in the rolling hills of central west Texas.

"Only that I always heard they shoot first and ask questions later," Ben said.

"Thanks," Clint said drily.

"You're plumb welcome."

Clint and Ben Adler rode slowly into the small ranching town. It looked like a thousand others Clint had seen in the west. One main street with a lot of false-fronted buildings on both sides, saloons mostly, but two general stores, a doctor's office and a funeral parlor. It was a simple, no-frills ranching community that gave the impression it had seen more bad times than good. They had passed a huge stockyard, empty of cattle now but in good repair. Clint looked for a sheriff's office but was not surprised when he saw none. He imagined that the Longely's were all the law they needed in town.

"What if we see this Rafe Longely and the Hathaway girl step out of a building or something?" Ben whispered.

Clint considered the possibility and decided it was unlikely such a thing would occur. And if it did, there was going to be hell to pay in a hurry. Since they had entered the town, they could feel the eyes of suspicious men watching them as they passed down the street. It was not a very comfortable feeling to know that their every move was being watched. Clint had taken the precaution of growing a beard in hopes that it would hide his true identity in case there were men here who would recognize him on sight. Unfortunately, the beard was still a little on the thin side yet.

"Well, goddammit, what would we do?" Ben demanded impatiently."

"I imagine, should that happen, we'd have two choices."

Ben waited. Finally, exasperated, he hissed, "Are you gonna tell me the choices, or what!"

"The first choice," Clint said, "would be whether or not we wanted Rafe to kill us or we kill him."

"And the second?"

Clint smiled. "Assuming we kill Rafe and make a grab for Milly, the second choice would be whether we surrender and get hung or get ourselves blown out of our saddles by some of these fellas who are studying us so closely."

Ben expelled a deep breath. "So you're saying that if we see Rafe now, we either get shot or hung."

"That would be about the size of it," Clint answered.

"Well, then, I sure hope we don't see them."

"Me too," Clint seconded. "It would have been a long ride for nothing."

Ben cussed under his breath. "I'll give you this much, Gunsmith, you're cold as steel under pressure."

At last they made their way to the livery and dismounted. Clint and Ben removed their saddlebags and left their weary horses to be grained, watered and groomed.

They had passed two small hotels on main street and since they both looked in about the same general state of decline, they headed for the nearest one.

Clint registered as Clint Evans from Evansville. Ben registered under his own name and hometown. The hotel clerk studied the entries for a moment and said,

"Evansville, New Mexico? Never even heard of it."

"Used to be called Santa Rosa."

"Oh, yeah! I heard of Santa Rosa. Say, that was a pretty name. Why'd they change it?"

"Long story," Clint said. "Why'd they name Longely, Longely?"

"Glad you asked. This town and the land it sits on was homesteaded by the Longely family years ago. They gave it to the town in exchange for a percentage of all profits. Better deal for them than for us. Profits are pretty skinny in these parts. Cattle prices are down, there's been a drought for almost two years now. You get enough rain over in New Mexico?"

"Yep."

The clerk nodded. He was a big man, the kind who looked like he ought to be a blacksmith rather than work a hotel desk. "What about up in the panhandle country?"

"A little dry," Ben said.

"Well, we need the rain," the clerk said with a sad shake of his head. "Cattle got to drink. What you boys here for?"

"Just passing through. Horses are a little played out and need to be reshod. Thought we might play a little poker and maybe win some money."

"There's always a couple of games going on. Small stakes, though, 'cept after payday on the ranches around the first of the month. You want a bath with the room?"

"Yeah," Clint said. "Two baths. Two rooms."

The clerk chuckled. "Gettin' a little sick of the sight and the smell of each other, huh?"

"That's about the size of it," Clint said. "Is the Longely family still ranching here in these parts?"

"Hell yes! Most everyone here is related in one way or another to the family. I'm not, that's why I'm working this crummy old desk job instead of something where I can earn some decent money."

"Where's their ranch headquarters?"

"About ten miles to the south. Why?"

"Just wondering."

"You ain't the law in disguise, are you?" the clerk asked suspiciously.

Ben snorted. "Do we look like law?"

"No," the man admitted. "You look too damn respectable for being the law. Besides, even the Texas rangers steer wide of Longely."

"That right?"

"Sure. They found it ain't too healthy. We had a ranger come riding in here about six months ago. He was sniffin' around and asking too many questions."

"What happened to him?" Ben asked.

"He just disappeared one night." The clerk looked at each of them. "Happens around here when folks ask too many damn fool questions. Now, gents, why are you really here?"

"Don't ask," Clint said, his voice going hard. "We just heard that this was a town where men on the run could find a little breathing room. Maybe sell a head or two of horses if there was a small question of doubt as to the real legal owner."

The clerk relaxed and smiled. "That's exactly the truth of it." He gave them their room keys. "You boys breath easy a couple of days and then you might want to look for work hereabouts. The Longelys are always looking for enterprising cowboys. And you both look enterprising. Am I readin' it right?"

Clint caught the drift right away and it was the kind

of opening he'd hoped he might hear. "You are, mister. And we hope you might pass along to whoever it is that we need to do some business right away."

"Eli Longely will probably be calling on you," the clerk said. "Until then, enjoy your rooms and baths."

Clint took his key and moved down the hall. He had no idea who this Eli fella was. Maybe he was Rafe's brother or even his father. Could be a cousin. One thing was sure, Clint knew he and Ben were going to have to find Rafe and Milly and get the hell out of this town before very long. Staying in Longely was like carrying around a lighted stick of dynamite in your back pocket —you knew that it was going to explode real soon but you could never pinpoint the exact moment.

TWENTY-EIGHT

That evening Clint and Ben visited the saloons and kept their ears and eyes wide open. Clint was always careful to keep his back to the wall and his hat pulled down low over his eyes. He and Ben sipped beer and positioned themselves at a back table where they could watch everyone coming and going. Each time the batwing doors of the saloon swung open, Clint would feel his body tense up, and when he saw that the man entering was a stranger, he relaxed. It was funny, but Ben was almost as nervous.

"I can't understand why we just don't ask where this Rafe fella is and go get the girl."

"Because," Clint said, "the minute we ask is the minute someone would go tell Rafe about us."

"We got to do something," Ben complained. "I sure can't see sitting around here waiting for someone to recognize you, beard or no beard."

"Maybe you're right," Clint admitted. "Got any money?"

"About a dollar is all."

"Are you any good at poker?"

"Damn good," Ben said with conviction.

Clint gave the young Texan five of his own dollars. "I'll watch from over here in case the game is rigged or anyone is doing any signaling. You do the playing."

"Am I supposed to win or lose?"

"Win, of course. But also see if you can find out if Rafe and Milly are staying at the Longely headquarters."

"I'll do it."

An hour later, Ben came back to the table with two more beers. "I lost all but two bits of your money. These boys sure know how to play cards."

"They probably used a marked deck. Any luck with where Rafe and Milly are staying?"

"Yeah. They're at the main ranch headquarters just like you figured. But from what I gathered, the place is heavily guarded by dogs that bark whenever anyone comes within a mile of the place."

"Then we'd never reach Milly without raising the alarm," Clint said.

"It appears we won't have to. Miss Hathaway and Rafe are coming into town a week from Sunday to get married. I heard the entire county is going to be here and the celebrating starts early."

Clint leaned forward with excitement. "That's perfect!" he whispered. "All we have to do is snatch her when she's getting dressed in her wedding gown."

Ben snapped his fingers. "Just like that, huh?"

"Just like that. They won't be expecting anything."

But Ben wasn't too happy with the plan. "I hate like hell to sit around for a whole week," he complained.

"Maybe we won't have to. They might bring her in to try on a wedding dress or something. We'll just have to keep a sharp eye out."

Ben looked glum. "I just want to get this done with and then outdraw and shoot you. After that, I can get on with my life back in Amarillo."

"Life is hard sometimes," Clint said. "But unless

you have any better ideas, we're going to just have to wait it out and hope for the best.''

"Gunsmith?"

"What?"

"Has it every occurred to you that this Miss Hathaway might have had a change of heart and actually want to marry this fella?"

Clint shook his head. "He robbed and murdered Milly's father. Ace Hathaway was a good man. No, Ben. Milly isn't going to be a smiling bride. They'll have to beat her to the altar and . . ."

"Evening, strangers," the cowboy said as he came to a stop at their table. "Enjoying yourselves?"

"Nice place," Clint said, noticing how the man's hands were all crusted with callouses and his face was burned a deep coppery brown. He wore big spurs and bat-wing chaps. He chewed tobacco and spit on the floor without thought of using a cuspidor. His was the longest handlebar mustache that Clint had ever seen on a man. His Stetson was shapeless, his eyes pale and very clear. When he came to a halt before their table, his knees remained a good four inches apart, making him look like he was astraddle an invisible horse. He was cowboy enough to step right off the front page cover of a western dime novel.

"My name is Eli Longely. Nate, the clerk over at the hotel, he said you boys was looking for some kind of money-making proposition. That right?"

"That's right."

"You any good at driving horses or cattle?"

"Been doing it right steady," Clint said.

"You ever carry your own branding iron?" Eli asked quietly.

Clint took a deep breath. "I figure a man has to make his own breaks in this world. Don't you, Ben?"

Ben just nodded.

"So do I," Eli said. "That's why me and a few of the boys are going to take a little ride into New Mexico starting early tomorrow morning. Gonna do a little horse gathering. I could use two extra hands. Men who can ride hard and shoot straight. Interested?"

Clint knew that they had to be interested. A man either joined this kind or fought them. "You bet we are," Clint said. "How much money might we be earning?"

"Fair question but one I'm afraid I can't answer," Eli said. "I've got a line on this band of horses we plan to take but until they're sold, you'll be paid a dollar a day."

"We'll take it."

"But what about the wedding!"

Eli glanced sideways at Ben. "What the hell has that got to do with you?" he demanded.

Ben almost swallowed his tongue and Clint had a strong urge to feed it to him along with his teeth. "Well, I just heard that the whole town will be celebrating. Sounded like a good time to me. That's all."

Eli studied him for a minute and then nodded. He smiled slowly. "It will be the biggest blowout since Pa and Ma got married back in 1845. Whole town stayed drunk a week. This time, it might even be better. We're bringing in two freightloads of whiskey and champagne all the way from Galveston Bay. There'll be some gals coming in to work and they'll be paid by the family so it'll be free for the taking."

Ben smiled. "That's what I heard. That's why I wanted to be here."

"Being here ain't hardly enough," Eli said. "You have to be invited to the party. And the only people who gets invited are the ones I say gets invited."

He pointed a finger at both Clint and Ben. "You boys prove as tough as you look, you'll be invited."

"Thanks," Clint said. "What time do we leave?"

Eli waved to the bartender for three more beers. "About midnight," he said. "We gather and ride out from the ranch headquarters."

Ben and Clint exchanged quick glances and they read each other's minds instantly. Was Rafe coming along on this little raid into New Mexico? And if not, would he at least be there to see them ride out? And even if he wasn't, what would they do when it came time to steal horses and maybe kill good men doing it? These and a dozen more questions filled Clint's mind as they sat and talked with Eli Longely a few more minutes until he got up and sauntered back to the bar.

"I think we've heard enough for now," Clint said. "Maybe we better go get a few hours of rest while we can. This might be a long, hard trip."

"We already been on one," Ben said.

"So we'll take another."

They nodded good night to Eli and the bartender and then headed down the street toward their hotel. It was a warm, almost balmy night and Clint couldn't help but wonder how Milly was doing. It was hard, real hard knowing she was within ten miles and yet he could not possibly help her for another week. And if something went wrong and they didn't get back in time for the wedding, what then?

Clint shook his head. He and Ben would get back in time come hell or high water—if Rafe wasn't planning to ride along on their damned horse-thief trail back to New Mexico.

TWENTY-NINE

Eli and a dozen men departed from Longely at about ten o'clock that night. Clint and Ben waited an hour before they followed. The idea was that they wanted as little as possible to do with Eli and his men until they were headed out for New Mexico. And the last thing they needed was for Eli to introduce them to the other horse thieves.

When they reached the Longely Ranch gate, they were stopped by two riflemen who stepped out from behind the trees and shouted, "Who are you?"

Clint stated their names and the reason for their visit. Fortunately, the riflemen waved them past and slipped back into the trees.

"Not a very friendly way to greet strangers, is it?" Ben said.

"These aren't very friendly people," Clint said. "And if Rafe sees us tonight, we might just as well shuck our guns and go down shooting because it'll be our last dance in this lifetime."

"Well, we just can't let him see us then!" Ben said. "We can stay in the darkest shadows until it's time to ride out. The thing that has me worried is, what do we do if this Rafe fella decides to come along?"

Clint just shrugged his shoulders. "It's always

157

worked best for me to just take things as they come. No sense worrying about something that might not even happen."

Ben shook his head. "I sure don't see how you survived all the scrapes and gun battles you was supposed to have won. Not the way you ride into a fix with no plan or anything."

"There are lots of folks who plan their whole lives out, Ben. They plan just what they're going to say and do. Who they'll marry and how they will get rich. I never met a one of them that stuck to any kind of plan. Life is just too damn full of twists and turns to map out."

Ben rode along in silence as the neared the Longely Ranch headquarters. "Maybe there's a lot of truth in what you just said and maybe it's all air. All I know is that you killed my brother and I plan to even the score."

"Your brother drew first. I killed him in order to stay alive. You can't fault a man for that, Ben."

"Yes I can," he said tightly. "And if these Longelys don't kill you before this is all settled, I will."

Clint took a deep breath. "Just put your mind on saving Milly Hathaway and the rest will take care of itself. When we get in among them, you do the talking. Someone might recognize me but your face won't mean anything to them."

They entered the ranchyard. Ben murmured under his breath, "Look at the size of this place!"

"It's a big one alright. It would take a hell of a lot of rustled cattle and horses to build a house like that."

The ranch house was two stories, with three big brick chimneys sticking out of the roof. Painted white and built of rock and wood, it was imposing.

And right now it was also ablaze with lanterns hanging off a front porch packed with men and women whom Clint judged to be the most important of the Longelys. An old, old man was playing a fiddle and he was very good. Tables laden with food covered a real grass lawn in front of the porch. Eli and his cowboys were eating off good china plates and drinking whiskey from crystal water goblets. Everyone was laughing and talking at once and having a high old time just as if it were broad daylight and a Sunday picnic. The entire scene was unreal but then, Clint had never met a wealthy outlaw family like this. He supposed this was how they normally behaved.

A soft breeze made the lanterns wave and their swaying light made the front porch seem like the rocking deck of a sailing ship.

"What do we do now?" Ben asked, slightly unnerved by the size of the crowd.

"You get two plates and fill 'em while I stand back outa the way and hold the horses," Clint said in a low voice. "Just act like everyone else is acting. Behave like you're having a high old time and planning on making a pile of money this week."

"Alright."

They dismounted out in the yard and kept the mass of horses and cowboys between themselves and the porch. While Ben sauntered through the throng toward the tables laden with food and drink, Clint held the horses and tried to see if Milly Hathaway was among the women seated on the big porch. He stood on his toes, his arms on his saddle, body hidden behind Duke. One by one, he studied the women until he decided that Milly was not among them. So far, Rafe was nowhere in sight.

Clint didn't know whether to be grateful or not. When Ben brought the food back, he ate despite the fact he had little appetite. He was just finishing up when he heard a scream and saw Rafe come busting out of the house dragging Milly behind. She was fighting him, yelling like a Comanche.

Clint started forward but Ben grabbed his arm tightly. "Don't," the younger man hissed. "You'll only get us killed and not help her a whit!"

"You're learning fast, kid." Clint made himself relax even when he saw Rafe pull Milly into his arms and kiss her, then shove her roughly aside.

Rafe lifted his long arms to the night sky as if he were praying for rain. "Alright!" he shouted, "Listen up! Pa, put down that goddamn old fiddle and hear me good."

No one was listening harder than the Gunsmith or Ben Adler, because they were about to find out if Rafe was leading this horse-stealing expedition or not.

"We've planned this raid out better than any before. You boys are going to 'borrow' some of the finest horses in New Mexico. And when you come back, there will be a wedding and a celebration the likes of which the Hill country hasn't seen in twenty-five years!"

Milly stepped in front of him. "The hell there will!" she screamed. "Not if it includes . . ."

She never finished. A huge old woman grabbed Milly by the hair and jerked her screaming and fighting into the house. They heard a table crash and then the old woman hollered, "I'll hide you, girl!"

Ben leapt forward but this time it was the Gunsmith who maintained control. "Don't!" he said with harsh urgency. That single word was enough to freeze Ben in his tracks. In the swaying lamplight, his face was etched as hard as polished stone.

Clint eased his grip on the young Texan's shoulder.

"I know," he said. "I feel the same way. But it will have to wait another week."

Rafe took a swig of whiskey right out of the battle. He stuck his head in the front door and said, "You don't hurt her, Ma. I want her to look the same way she looked when I brung her here!"

He drank again, wiped his mouth with the back of his hand and turned back to face the crowd. "My bride-to-be and I will be looking to buy a ranch this week and take care of all the arrangements to make this a real celebration."

Eli yelled, "If Ma don't kill her! Are you ever gonna tame that she-wolf, Rafe?"

Everyone laughed except the Gunsmith and Ben.

"Yeah, on our wedding night I damn sure will!" Rafe bragged. "By the next morning, she'll be meowing like a little kitten wantin' my milk!"

Again, laughter and applause while the Gunsmith clenched his teeth in helpless anger and frustration. It was maddening to think about leaving Milly for another week of this hell. But there was no choice.

Eli turned to the cowboys. "We'll be riding out in about half an hour so everyone finish up your eating and drinking and bring your plates, glasses and forks inside to the kitchen. Ma says she'd hide the man who breaks any glassware. Then I want you to check your guns and ammunition."

Clint finished his plate and when Ben was done, he said, "Give it to me."

"I'll take them up to the house," Ben said.

Clint hesitated. He'd decided that he had to let Milly know she was not abandoned, that there was hope. But if he went into the house and someone recognized him in it's bright interior, the game was over.

"Alright," he said reluctantly as he gave Ben his empty plate. "Tell Milly that we're starting off tonight for New Mexico but we'll be back before the wedding and get her away from here."

"Can I tell her we might even come right back?"

"No," Clint said. "It'd be better if we just let her think we'll be gone all week. Otherwise, she might start acting like any minute we could appear. Rafe could get suspicious."

"Anything else I should tell her?"

Clint thought about it for a minute. "Tell her not to let Rafe buy a ranch with her father's money. Stall him. We may have to leave Texas on the run and, if we do, I don't want that girl to be left penniless. Tell her to find out where Rafe keeps all his money."

"What if he's already deposited it in the Longely bank?"

"Uh-uh," Clint said. "I've never known an outlaw yet that trusted a bank with his money. No, Rafe will have poor old Ace Hathaway's money stashed away somewhere close at hand."

THIRTY

Ben's hands were shaking and the dishes and glasses rattled together as he carried them up to the porch. A girl about sixteen, who might have been pretty except for buck-teeth, saw him and smiled.

"What's your name, handsome?"

Ben was not accustomed to such boldness in a girl but then, he'd never met the daughter of a pack of outlaws. "Ben," he said.

"Well, Ben, my name is Darlene and if you make it back to the ranch, I want to dance with you some at the wedding reception."

"Be my pleasure," Ben said, stepping up on the crowded porch and trying to reach the front.

"I'll take those dishes inside for you," Darlene said, reaching for them.

"Awhh," he said, trying desperately to think of something that would allow him access to the inside of the house. "I heard this place is so nice, I sorta wanted to see it for myself."

Darlene seemed pleased. She leaned close and whispered in his ear. "If'n you'd come up into the light earlier this evening so I could see your face, I'd have invited you to see the inside of my bedroom."

Ben was so shocked he almost dropped his plates.

"I heard that, Darlene!" a woman Ben supposed was the girl's mother screeched as she slapped the girl with the open palm of her hand. "Shameless hussy!"

The hand struck the side of Darlene's face and she howled, then raced inside and up the stairs crying. The woman said, "You stay away from her, you good-lookin' sonofabitch!"

"Yes, ma'am!" Ben said, as he pushed inside and headed for the kitchen. He could scarcely believe his good fortune when he saw Milly alone, washing dishes in a big soapy tub of water. "Afraid I got some more for you, Miss."

She turned to see him and he noticed how her eyes were all puffy from crying. She looked pale and unwell but there was also a spark of anger and defiance that burned brightly in her eyes. "Just drop them in the tub and go about your business, cowboy."

He dropped them into the steaming tub and knelt beside it for a minute. What he wanted to do most of all was take this young lady's hand and race out the back door of the house and run away. But that was a crazy impulse so he just said, "Milly, the Gunsmith and I are going to take you home next week."

Milly was washing a big platter and when he said those words, it fell from her hand and would have shattered on the floor if Ben had not reacted instantly and caught it an inch off the ground. She stared at him, her eyes growing round with hope and wonder. "You mean it!" she breathed.

"I swear it on my life," Ben said with a broad smile. "The Gunsmith would have come in himself only he was afraid he might get recognized, even with a beard."

Tears sprang into her eyes. She dropped the platter into the soapy water and started to reach out and hug him but Ben jumped away. "Don't you cry or do that, Miss Hathaway. If someone was to walk in here and see us, it'd be a real mess."

Milly nodded her head then used her apron to dry her eyes. "You're right," she whispered. "It's just that I'm so damned happy to see that someone has finally come to help me."

"Gunsmith says to get ahold of your daddy's money that Rafe stole. Be ready to leave fast."

"But when . . . " The light in her eyes died. "Hello, Rafe."

He seemed surprised and overjoyed that she would even greet him. "Did Ma hurt you, honey?"

"Not any more this time than usual."

Rafe nodded, then glared at Ben. "You got glue stuck to the bottoms of your boots, cowboy? Or what!"

Ben's cheeks flushed hotly. He wanted to kill this man but instead, he just nodded humbly and said, "Thanks for the food, Miss. Pleasure meeting you."

Milly lifted her chin and looked right into his eyes. "Thanks for bringing me . . . the dishes."

Ben turned away feeling as if his heart was going to burst in his chest. He stumbled outside thinking he had just seen the prettiest and bravest young woman in the world. The way she spoke, so calm and trusting. The way her eyes met his and, oh, Christ, he thought, miserably, I'll never have a girl like that! Not only do we have to save her from that big murdering bastard that plans to marry her, but she must be in love with the Gunsmith. And I'm going to kill him and that'll make her hate me.

"Did you speak with her?" Clint asked excitedly the moment his partner returned.

"Yep." Ben tightened his cinch.

"Well, what did she say?"

"She said thanks."

"That's all?"

Ben glared at the Gunsmith. "What else did you expect her to say in there!" Ben almost shouted.

Clint curbed his own anger. Just when he thought he understood this kid and began to like him, Ben started acting up again. Clint looked at Ben closely and saw that the young man from Amarillo looked like he'd swallowed something that had left a real sour taste in his mouth.

And then, the Gunsmith understood. He's smitten with Milly! That would explain it. Clint reached out and slapped his young friend on the shoulder. "Cheer up," he said, tightening his own cinch as the riders mounted up to ride into New Mexico. "Milly hasn't been wed by anyone yet."

Ben looked at him kind of funny. "She loves you, don't she?"

"Yes. But . . ."

"You gonna marry her if we get through this?"

"How could I marry her if you kill me?"

"Some kind of fluke could happen," Ben said slyly. "You could kill me, I guess."

"Stranger things have happened." Clint mounted Duke.

Ben mounted his own horse. "If you killed me, would you marry her? I want to know, dammit!"

Clint studied the young man. "No. At least not right away," he answered as he reined Duke around and started after the others.

THIRTY-ONE

They galloped across the muddy Pecos River and into
the rugged Guadalupe Mountains that trickle into the
southeast corner of New Mexico. It was tough country,
covered with more sage than grass. It was Apache country, and those that came and settled in it were fighting
men and women.

The cattle and mining town of La Rosa was as hard-
looking as a tired old whore and just as unappealing.
There was one bank, a sheriff's office, six saloons and
one hotel besides the other usual establishments.

"We'll rest ourselves and our horses here for the
night," Eli said as they entered the town. "I don't want
to get ahold of something we can't run away from because of spent horses."

"How far is the Rocking B Ranch from here?"

"About twenty miles north. We can ride up there and
hit them tomorrow night and be fifty miles toward
Texas by the following morning. This is Sheriff Jesse
Drago's town. We want to behave ourselves and be
peaceable. No trouble. Pass the word. Any man ar-
rested by Drago is outa a job and on his own. He says
anything about the rest of us, he's gonna be dead."

Clint eased himself down from the saddle. He had
wrapped his broken forearm tightly with a two-inch
strip of leather and, with his shirtsleeve buttoned down

to his wrist, his injury was not even evident. The arm
was healing well. It bothered him only if he forgot about
it and did something stupid like try to lift a heavy object.

Clint was smiling inwardly. Jesse Drago. Sonofagun!
Old Jesse must be sixty-five years old. Clint thought the
man had retired or been bushwhacked years ago. Jesse
was one of the West's last great sheriffs, a legend among
lawmen even though his fame was not well publicized.
Outlaws gave Jesse Drago a wide berth because he was
the kind of man that shot first and then read his victims
their rights. Jesse was a crusty old sonofabitch who
could smell out danger and trouble as if he had a sixth
sense for it. He had as good a survival instinct as any
man that Clint had ever known.

The Texans stabled their weary horses and paired off
so as not to attract any attention. In towns like this, any
body of unknown horsemen was justifiably viewed with
suspicion. They might just be a crew of drovers or
hunters, but it was also true that they could just as easily
be bank or stagecoach robbers.

Clint and Ben had dinner early. After dark, Clint
took his friend aside and said, "I got an old friend I
want you to meet." Ben hadn't been very communi-
cative since leaving Milly. The young man was clearly
distracted by his own troubled thoughts. So far, Clint
just hadn't seen an opportunity to explain that, while he
felt a strong attachment to Milly Hathaway, he felt an
equally strong attachment to the status of bachelor-
hood.

"Who would that be?"

"Jesse Drago," Clint said. "I think it's time we got
ourselves a little help from some friends."

Ben perked up. "You know Drago?"

"We fought together at the Battle of Box Springs

about twelve years ago. You probably heard of that fight.''

"Who hasn't?" Ben asked. "We gonna get Sheriff Drago to help us?"

Clint nodded. "I think he'd be real put out if I didn't invite him, don't you?"

"Well, I guess!"

Getting to Jesse Drago without being seen by Eli or one of his horse thieves was easy. They just waited until the old lawman stepped outside to make his nightly rounds of the saloons and then they hailed him from the safe darkness of a side alley.

"Drago!"

The lawman had been shambling along the boardwalk looking half asleep, but when Clint called his name from the shadows, the old boy proved he was still dangerous. He dropped to one knee and his gun seemed to leap into his hands as he called, "Who's there?"

"The Gunsmith!" Clint whispered. "Put that old blunderbuss back where it belongs and don't make such a show. I need to talk to you without being seen."

Drago shoved his gun into his holster. He brushed the dust from his knee, acted as if he had stumbled, and then continued to shuffle down the boardwalk.

"Where's he going?" Ben asked.

"He'll make his usual rounds in case anyone is watching, then he'll double back through the alley and come up on us from behind. Just pretend that you're caught by surprise. It sorta tickles the old bastard to think he's just as stealthy as an Apache. Truth is, he's shot guns so long that it's affected his hearing."

It took Drago nearly an hour to get in behind them, and when he did, they heard him coming pretty nearly five minutes before he cocked his gun and said, "Freeze up and turn around slow, hands over your heads."

They did as they were ordered. Jesse used his thumb-nail to strike a match and then he held it up to their faces. "You don't look like the Gunsmith to me."

"I grew this beard to hide my identity." Clint grinned and said, "Who else but me would know that, at Box Springs, you really did kill two Apache with an old Sharps buffalo rifle whose broken stock you wrapped in rawhide?"

Drago allowed himself a toothless smile that was more unnerving to most men than reassuring. He snuffed the match out and holstered his gun saying, "Gunsmith! Goddamit! What the blazes are you doing hiding in an alley?"

"I need your help. We've got most of the Longely family from Texas with us tonight. We're going to raid a place called the Rocking B Ranch tomorrow night and steal a few horses. Thought you might like to know about it."

"Well sonofabitch!" Drago said with delight. "I ain't had any action to speak of around here in almost a six months! This is good news!"

"Same old Jesse Drago," Clint said proudly.

"Who's the green kid you got tagging along by your apron strings?" Drago asked, squinting in the moon-light.

"He's come to help. Wants to kill me after this is all settled, but for now, he's on our side."

If Jesse Drago was confused by this explanation, he did not show it. He just said, "Boy, you kill the Gun-smith, I'll kill you."

Ben didn't say a word.

"We'd better go back to the saloon and put in an-other appearance," Clint said. "We're leaving early but holing up somewheres near the ranch and going after those horses after dark."

"Those will be the horses that Judge Smith bought for the U.S. Cavalry. About two hundred of them, all sound and broke to ride. Those kinds of horses are always worth a lot of money."

"Jesse, I'll see you there," Clint said as he started to leave.

"Wait a minute," Ben cried. "It'll be darker'n hell out there. How is he and is men going to know us from Eli and the others?"

Drago spat tobacco and drawled, "Not entirely a dumb question, Gunsmith. Tell you what. Shoot the leader and a couple of them when we attack and then clear the hell out. We'll take care of the rest."

"Sounds good," Clint said. "And if it's all right with you, I'll give my thanks now. There's a wedding we need to get back to in a big hurry."

"Well, congratulations, Gunsmith!" Drago slapped Clint on the shoulder hard enough to rock him back on his bootheels.

"It's not mine," Clint said.

"Then . . ."

"It's a long story and I'll tell it to you next time I pass through," Clint told the sheriff as he shook the man's hand. "Tomorrow night it's gonna be like old times again, eh, Jesse."

The lawman chuckled. "Just like. You always did bring excitement trailing along on your coattails, Gunsmith!"

Clint turned and walked away. Old Jesse was like a firehorse when it heard the sound of the fire bells. There weren't many men like Jesse Drago left in this world. And that was a damn shame.

THIRTY-TWO

They stood beside their horses under the cottonwood trees. Fourteen men, ten of them Longely men. All afternoon they had waited patiently for Eli's scouts to return with news of exactly where the horses they intended to steal were being kept. If they were found in the main corrals near the ranch house, it might mean that there would be a hard gunfight. But if the horses were being kept farther out, then perhaps they could steal them under the cover of darkness and make their getaway without firing a shot.

Ben was nervous. He had found it hard to sit or stand in one place. Twice, Eli had told him to "sit on your tailbone and stay put!" But it wasn't easy and there were several of the Longely men who were every bit as fidgety.

But now, as the sun dipped toward the western mountains and the shadows raced out from the trees, the scouts were returning on foot. Everyone rushed to them and they looked tired and grim-faced.

Matt Longely, the leader of the two scouts, said, "Eli, the horses are all being kept in the ranch corrals but everybody seems to be out on roundup."

Eli was not pleased. "They might come back tonight."

"There's no way of knowin'," Matt said. "The only

folks I could see all afternoon there was an old China-man doing laundry in the back and another old cook.''

"No women?''

"Nope.''

Eli rubbed his stubbled cheeks. "Was the cook cookin' a big dinner?''

The scout frowned. "How'm I supposed to know that or not?''

"Did you see a big fire and smoke coming out of the cookshack!''

The two scouts looked at each other and began to shake their heads.

"Good!'' Eli said. "That must mean the cowboys and their bosses are out on the range. Maybe hunting wild horses or cattle. Let's ride in, get those horses and ride out.''

"What about the cook and the Chinaman?'' Clint asked softly. "I wouldn't want to leave any witnesses.''

"Good thinking. You and the kid take care of them permanently.''

"Be easier if you'd give us at least a five minute headstart. That way, we can sneak in and take care of them so there's no chance of any shooting. The sound of gunfire carries a long ways. The Chinaman would probably just hide someplace, but the old cook might grab a rifle and give us fits.''

"All right,'' Eli conceded. "You got five minutes. But I know what you got in mind.''

Clint felt himself stiffen. "You do?''

"Sure. You're going to try and find some jewelry or money. Well, whatever you find is gonna be split be-tween all of us.''

"Now wait a minute,'' Clint said belligerently.

Eli held up his hand for silence. "I just decided that I don't trust either of you enough to send you on in there

alone. I'm coming with you to make sure you don't try
to hide some diamonds or something.''

"Good idea, Eli," one of the brothers said, shooting
an unfriendly look at Clint. "They ain't proved themselves loyal to us yet."

Clint knew when it was time to shut his mouth and
give in. Further argument would only raise suspicions.
He just hoped that Ben would decide to do the same. He
was pleased when Ben turned to his horse and mounted
without comment.

Eli said, "You boys give us about ten minutes and
don't come into the ranchyard until I wave a bandana
through the window. I want no shooting or noise, just
drive those horses outa those corrals and run the daylights outa them for Texas. With luck, nobody will even
know we came and went until tomorrow."

It took them less than twenty minutes to reach the
ranch headquarters. The Smith house was wood and it
had nice lead-glass windows and solid doors with fine
etchings. Anyone could see that Judge Smith was doing
right well for himself.

"Alright," Eli said, "we leave the horses here in these
trees and walk to the back door of the house. Once inside, we kill the Chinaman and the cook and then we see
if we can find a safe."

"So what if we do?" Clint asked.

Eli rubbed his calloused fingers against his thumbs.
"I know these horny old paws don't look like much, but
they can pick a lock or open a safe right well. I used to
make my living cracking safes in Chicago."

"Hmmm," Clint said. "I'd never have guessed."

As they entered the house through the kitchen, Clint
was more than a little curious about what they'd find.
He hoped it would be Jesse Drago and a crowd of heavily armed men.

Suddenly, the cook ambled inside and was caught completely unaware. He was carrying a pail of water and when he saw Clint, Ben and Eli, he yelled, threw his water at them and took off running.

"Kill him!" Eli shouted. "Don't let him get to the front door!"

Ben was the youngest among them and he tackled the cook in the entryway while the man put up a hell of a fight. Eli stormed in and yelled, "Get off of him, Ben! Give me a clear shot!"

"Yiiiip Oooochooowww!" the Chinaman screamed as he vaulted into the hallway wielding a big meat cleaver. Clint heard the steel whistle through the air. He ducked and Eli caught the blow on his upraised forearm. The outlaw screamed in pain and grabbed his wound to stop the heavy flow of blood. His six-gun clattered to the floor.

"Shoot them both!" Eli hissed through clenched teeth.

It was all Clint could do to throw himself back out of the Chinaman's way as another blow missed his nose by mere inches.

Clint drew his gun and pointed it right at the man. "Drop it you crazy bastard or I'll shoot!"

"Yiipp Ouchooow!" the chinaman howled as he attacked with renewed intensity. He swung so hard the meat cleaver missed Clint's head and buried itself in the doorway. He tried frantically to pull it free and that's when Clint rapped his skull with the barrel of his Colt revolver. The Chinaman went down to stay.

"Shoot the cook!" Eli gritted, his face pale.

"I can't do that," Clint said as Ben finally delivered a stunning blow to the older man's jaw that stiffened him up then put him out.

Eli stared at Clint. "What the hell . . . ."

"Find a rope, Ben, and tie this snake up before you try to stop him from bleeding to death."

Eli spluttered and then he reached inside his shirt and pulled a hide-out gun. Clint expected it, but Ben did not. The little gun came out and Eli would have shot Ben through the brain if Clint's foot hadn't swept up and sent the gun exploding toward the ceiling. Ben was so furious he punched Eli hard enough to break his jaw. The outlaw leader rolled over on his side and didn't move as Ben tied his hands and got a bandage on his forearm.

Clint moved quickly. He took his own bandana and waved it before the window muttering, "Where the hell are you, Drago!"

The Longely crowd of horse thieves came stampeding into the ranch yard. There wasn't much daylight remaining.

Clint stepped out on the porch and started across the yard. He still thought like a lawman. You couldn't arrest men without proof and the proof was in the taking of the judge's horses. Clint watched as the corrals were opened and when the horses were stampeded out, he drew his gun and yelled, "You're all under arrest!"

The outlaws looked at him like he was insane and, just as they were thinking he might be better off dead, good old Jesse Drago and five men almost as old and straight-shooting as himself charged out of the barn on horseback.

"Yeeehoooo!" Jesse shouted, drawing his gun and crying, "Drop your guns, you're all under arrest!"

But since horse thieves were hung in New Mexico as well as most everywhere else, the order was ignored. Clint hit the ground as bullets stitched through the dusty air. He began firing and when one man tried to drive his horse into him, the Gunsmith shot him out of the saddle. But it was over almost as fast as it began. Without Eli to lead them, the Longelys scattered like quail and were soon being shot or captured. Clint stayed right in the yard and did his share until there was nothing else moving. He could still hear, somewhere far to the east, old Drago's wild battle cry.

Clint and Ben finished tying and patching up the outlaws who were still alive. A couple of Drago's old friends returned to take over.

"Tell Jesse I'll be seeing him again," Clint said.

"You mean you're jest ridin' off right now?"

Clint looked at Ben. They were both thinking about Milly Hathaway. And what if just one of the horse-thieving Longely's had escaped in the fading light? What if he managed to reach Longely before Clint and Ben could rescue Milly?

"Yeah," Clint said as he and Ben headed for the trees to retrieve their horses. "This is only half finished."

When they reached their horses and started to swing into their saddles, Ben said, "If you aren't going to marry her right away, then I'm going to ask for her hand as soon as I see her next."

A wry grin split Clint's lips. "She'll turn you down. Milly has some pretty set ideas about the kind of man she wants to marry."

"Hell," Ben said with a trace of a smile. "She can't be that all-fired fussy. She wants to marry you, don't she?"

Despite the circumstances and the urgency of their reaching Longely, Texas, in time to stop the wedding, Clint had to laugh.

THIRTY-THREE

They rode back across the Pecos River and when they discovered the tracks of a running horse, both Clint and Ben had the same sinking feeling that one of the Longely men had escaped.

Clint rested his gelding and let the animal cool down. "If they're warned, it just means we'll have a welcoming committee waiting for us in Longely."

Ben nodded bleakly. "It could mean that half the town will be waiting. Gonna make it damn hard to get Miss Hathaway outa there, Gunsmith."

Clint retightened his cinch and stepped into his stirrup. His left arm was feeling a lot better and he guessed it was nearly healed. It would have been healed completely if Juliet hadn't fallen on it while they were making love. When he thought about her, Clint got a warm feeling in the hollow of his stomach. Maybe, maybe if they survived this scrape, he'd let Ben return Milly to Evansville while he moseyed back up to Amarillo and paid that lovely, but clumsy, café owner a long visit.

"Gunsmith?" Ben asked. "Whatcha smilin' for?"

Clint pulled his thoughts back to the present. "It's not important," Clint said.

When the lone rider came pounding into the ranchyard, Milly heard the commotion. She came outside on the porch and listened as Rafe's youngest cousin, Harry Longely, told his story.

"It was the same two sonsofbitches Eli hired in the saloon!" Harry swore. "I don't know who they were. But they betrayed us to the law. I'm the only one that got out of there alive!"

Ma Longely wailed and began to get crazy. Pa Longely cursed a vicious blue streak and Rafe raged helplessly before he shouted, "Describe them to me!"

"The younger one was about six foot, black, wavy hair. Good-looking bastard about twenty, maybe twenty-one years old."

Rafe spun around and grabbed Milly. "He was the one talking to you in the kitchen!"

"So what!" she cried.

Rafe stared at her. "What about the other man?"

Milly held her breath.

"The other one was about the same size and build but maybe ten years older. He was real quiet. Had a full beard so you couldn't really see his face that good. Eli thought he was alright. He rode a big, black gelding."

Rafe visibly paled. "Star on the forehead?"

"Yeah. But . . ."

"Describe his saddle and gun!"

Harry did so with some detail and when he was finished, Rafe said, "It's the Gunsmith. The bastard has come for Milly and me. Did you see Eli after the shooting started?"

"Nope. Only the other two Judas's along with that goddamn Jesse Drago and his posse. None of us had much of a chance. They caught us by surprise and killed half of us in the first volley of gunfire. Some of the others got run down. Only reason I got away is because

I had the fastest horse of the lot."

Ma Longely screamed hysterically and attacked poor Harry. She beat him off the porch with her fat fists and shrieked, "You should have fought to the death like the other boys! Goddamn you Harry!"

"But Ma! I wanted to warn you folks!"

"The hell you did! You was scared to death! You ran, you sniveling little bastard. Kill him Rafe, kill the boy!"

Rafe looked disgusted. He said, "Get her outa here, Pa. Pour a jug of whiskey down her gullet and, if that don't work, knock her alongside the head. Either way, put her to sleep."

Pa nodded and led his wife away.

"She wants me dead," Harry whispered in a broken voice.

Rafe took a deep breath and let it out slowly. "She's crazy. You did the right thing to come and warn me."

Harry nodded. "I heard of the Gunsmith. Maybe we oughta go into town and stay until we see if he's coming back to Texas."

"He's coming back alright," Rafe said. "He means to save Milly and me from our wedding."

"You're still gonna get married?"

Rafe nodded. He squeezed Milly tightly, one of his big hands cupped her breast possessively until she pulled it away. "You damn right we are. And that's gonna bring the Gunsmith right to us. I know his kind. This is a matter of honor to him. He can't let Miss Hathaway be wed and bed by me. Can he darling?"

Milly was filled with hatred and revulsion for this man. She struggled to break from his grasp but his strong arms bound her tight. "I'll never marry you!"

"Yes you will," Rafe said. "And it'll happen right in the middle of Longely. I want everybody to be there,

Harry. Tell them to be ready for a killing, a wedding and a celebration, in just that order."

Harry looked stunned. "But we already lost nine Longely men!"

"That's right. Just means that those of us who survived will have a little more of the pie to eat. Think of it that way, Harry."

Even Milly was shocked by the man's ruthless reasoning. She shuddered while vowing that, if Clint was drawn into a fatal trap and riddled by the Longely clan, she would kill Rafe on their wedding bed the moment he was unarmed.

THIRTY-FOUR

It was Sunday morning but the church bells weren't ringing. In fact, there was no church in Longely, Texas. Nor a school or a ladies club because the kids went uneducated and their mothers were certainly not ladies.

Clint and Ben were hidden upstairs in Room 201 of the Antelope Hotel. Behind them sat a prostitute named Della, a woman with hard, lifeless eyes and a thirst for revenge. Della had come to Longely, Texas, many years before and she had fallen in love with Rafe and dreamed of marrying him. But that all changed the night he got drunk. In a fit of anger Rafe had carved his initials in Della's right breast with the tip of his knife before leaving for New Mexico.

The ugly wounds had become infected and they left disfiguring scars, ones that could not be hidden despite the makeup Della wore so thickly to hide them. For all the years that Rafe had been working for Ace Hathaway, Della had alternately dreamed of killing Rafe and then, in fits of fancy, dreamed of having Rafe return to take her into his arms and tell her he was sorry and that she was still his woman and now he would marry her. After all, he had left his permanent marks on her and that would be the only honorable thing for such a man to do.

When Rafe finally returned, Della had bought a new dress and a gold necklace to make her look beautiful for him again. Before the scars, she had been beautiful. But then came the news that Rafe Longely had brought another woman to marry.

From that moment on, Della had lived only to see Rafe Longely dead.

"You could shoot him from this window," she said as she watched the pair. "It would be easy. Put a bullet through his heart. Or better yet, I'll do it."

Clint turned to face the woman. "Della," he said gently, "you swore you would not interfere but only help us save the woman. I told you that Rafe murdered her father and almost killed her brother."

"I swore not to interfere if you stopped the wedding. I would never allow that to take place. Maybe I should give his bride-to-be a gun. Does she have the stomach to put a bullet into that animal?"

"No," Clint said. "I don't think so. But I do."

"So do I," Ben said. "But we have to get Miss Hathaway out of there first. And they're looking for us."

Della studied them. "I could make you look like women. Tall women, but you could walk with bent knees and perhaps get close enough to save the girl."

Clint looked at Ben. The idea of putting on a wig and makeup was repugnant, but so far, he had not been able to see any way to get near Milly, who was heavily guarded.

"It might work."

Ben frowned. "Can't we think of something better?"

"I haven't been able to yet. Have you?"

Ben had to shake his head no.

"Time is running out on us. Alright, let's give it a try."

Della nodded. "There is only one condition. You must kill Rafe before he leaves that platform below. I will not allow him to take the woman to his bed."

"Neither will I," Clint said. "Alright. If something goes wrong and we're killed down there, I hope you put a bullet through his heart. But they'll see you and you'll be hanged—or worse."

Della smiled with a cold, bitter twist to her mouth. "It is of no concern what happens to me," she said. "So let's hurry and I will turn you both into shameless, ugly whores like me."

Clint started to protest but when he saw the dead eyes and hate-filled face of the woman, he changed his mind. Della was living in hell.

Rafe had found a man to play the role of a preacher. He was dressed in a black suit, white shirt and starched collar. He looked the part but when he opened the Bible to read, his hands were trembling and he kept mopping his face with a neckerchief.

Both Clint and Ben were standing in the crowd sweating profusely because of the thick wigs and heavy makeup they wore. They were also wearing shawls, big, frilly dresses and several petticoats to hide their definitely unfeminine physiques.

"Are you sure they'll pass through the crowd this way?" Ben whispered as the crowd grew restless and noisier by the minute. All around them there were men drinking out of bottles and shoving each other about.

"They ought to," Clint said tightly.

But a moment later, when a cheer arose from the crowd, Clint knew he'd misjudged the situation. Rafe, his parents and Milly came toward the platform from the wrong direction. Furthermore, they were being escorted by a body of heavily armed men.

Ben swore softly and Clint balled his fists at his sides and said, "We can't stop it. We'll have to get her away after the wedding ceremony."

"But . . ."

Clint leaned close to his young friend. "What does it matter!" he said in a low, urgent voice. "To do anything now would be suicide."

Ben nodded grimly.

The wedding party reached the platform and they climbed up and the preacher wasted no time beginning. Clint noticed right away that Milly looked faint and drugged. She was being supported by Rafe.

"What have they done to her?" Ben whispered.

"I don't know." Clint took a deep breath. The crowd became hushed and tense. They had expected Milly to put up a fight but there was none. They had also been warned that the famous Gunsmith would try to stop the ceremony. Men gripped their gunbutts in one hand, their bottles of cheap whiskey or rye in the other.

The preacher took courage as he neared the end of the marriage vows. "And so, if I hear no one who objects to this holy marriage between Mr. Rafus Longely and Miss Mildred Hathaway, I now pronounce you . . ."

"*I* object, you bloody bastard!"

All heads turned at the scream and they saw Della and her rifle. Rafe threw himself and Milly sideways off the platform to crash into the crowd below. Della began to work the rifle as fast as she could lever it and pull the trigger. Men scattered in wild panic. Clint and Ben alone sprinted toward the base of the wooden platform. Ben reached Milly first and he tore the drugged and almost unconscious girl out of Rafe's arms as Della's rifle bullets screamed around them.

"Hey, you . . ." Rafe jumped up with his gun in his hand and as the Gunsmith whirled, the hammer of his own gun caught in his cumbersome dress. Clint saw Rafe's pistol come up and he braced himself for the killing bullet he knew he could not prevent.

Suddenly, Rafe's mouth flew open. His tall body stiffened and he rose on the very tips of his toes. He took three short, mincing steps and Clint saw his stunned expression become vacuous. Della shot him a second time and Rafe was dead before he slammed facedown in the dirt. Clint's own gun came up and then he and Ben were dragging Milly away while confusion swept through the streets of Longely, as Della waged her own final battle.

Clint had planned an escape route through the big general store. Dashing inside, he and Ben tore off their wigs and women's clothing. They made a pile and Clint struck a match.

"Watch the front door and cover me!" Clint yelled as he lit a match that quickly ignited their hated disguises. The street outside was full of running men and gunfire. Ben shot at anyone who tried to enter while Clint grabbed a full bolt of calico cloth and dragged it the entire length of the store. The moment it caught fire, the cloth became a ribbon of flame that ignited a barrel of pine tar and exploded up the walls.

When the entire building was well on the way to becoming a raging inferno, Clint yelled, "Let's get out of here!"

There were four horses waiting behind the store and Duke was one of them.

"What about Della?" Ben cried, as they helped Milly into the saddle.

Clint grabbed his reins and swung onto his black gelding. "She's already dead," he told the younger man. "I don't think she's been alive for a long, long time."

They rode down the alley lighting pitch torches they'd already placed beside the back door of each establishment. Before they even reached the end of Longely, the flames from the general store were being joined by an entire line of new fires.

"It's done," Clint said when they pulled up a mile out of town to watch Longely burn. "In an hour there will be nothing left of this town but the ashes."

"Good riddance," Ben said.

Clint looked at the town and said, "Ben, take her back to Evansville where she belongs. Always take good care of her."

"What about you?"

"I'll guard your backtrail a few days just in case. When I'm sure that no one follows I'll come along."

"No you won't," Ben said. "But if you do, I'll still have to settle my score with you, Gunsmith."

Clint smiled wearily and scraped at the heavy makeup on his face. "Good-bye, Ben. Be a good man for her or I will come back and you'll have to make good on your brag."

For the first time, Ben seemed embarrassed by his obstinacy. He stuck his hand out and said, "Don't ever come back, Gunsmith. And I swear that if she marries me, I'll make her proud and happy. I give you my word on it."

"That's good enough for me," the Gunsmith said, his eyes thoughtful and sad for the disfigured prostitute who had died to save their lives.

Clint did not look back when Ben took Milly away. He would keep his own promise and remain on this trail until he was certain that no Longely was foolish enough to go to New Mexico. But none would. Rafe had been their leader and Rafe was dead.

He stepped down from his horse and rubbed Duke's ears affectionately as he watched the flames shoot toward the sky. "I'll tell you one thing, old friend, we're missing out on a hell of a wiener roast."